The Ghost of East Texas
Sequel to Terminal Event

Ali Spooner

The Ghost of East Texas
Sequel to Terminal Event

Ali Spooner

Affinity
Rainbow Publications

2021

The Ghost of East Texas
Sequel to Terminal Event
© 2021 by Ali Spooner

Affinity E-Book Press NZ LTD
Canterbury, New Zealand

1st Edition

ISBN: 978-1-98-858897-1

Editor: Angie Koenig
Proof Editor: Alexis Smith
Cover Design: Irish Dragon Design
Production Design: Affinity Publication Services

ACKNOWLEDGMENTS

I would like to thank my fans for following my stories, providing great feedback, and encouragement. Writing wouldn't be so much fun without you. Thanks to Affinity, Irish Dragon for the cover art and the team of editors, readers, and publishers who continue to help me grow as a writer.

DEDICATION

During the process of finishing this story, I learned of the passing of a dear friend. Grace Simpson, known to many as "Mama G," she will forever be in my heart. "Mama G" was very special to the "Affinity Girls" as she called us, and supported many authors in the Lesfic community. Trips to Texas will not be the same without her beautiful smile and quick wit to entertain us all. I can imagine her young and healthy, surrounded by dozens of cats as she watches over us. I miss and love you, "Mama G."

TABLE OF CONTENTS

CHAPTER ONE

FBI Special Agent Blair Cooper gathered her notes from the podium and placed them inside a small briefcase. She had just completed her presentation to a room filled with New York State Police on procedures for profiling serial murder cases. She was eager to wade through the crowd of participants and make her way home to Virginia. Blair shook several hands and accepted appreciation comments as she made her way through the large conference room. Blair grimaced at the bright sunlight as she walked outside, and quickly put on a pair of dark sunglasses to shield her eyes. After a short flight, Blair would be home. She and her lover and partner, Tally Rainwater, had plans to spend a long weekend at the coast to relax and rewind.

Since they met, three years earlier, on a case in the deep south, Blair and Tally had developed into a crime-fighting team. Tally had the gift of second sight that emerged in childhood, a gift that had been very useful in assisting Blair and the FBI in solving a serial killer case that struck very close to home for Tally. Her psychic skills were so accurate that the FBI enlisted her as a consultant to assist with investigations, and Tally and Blair had been consistently busy since returning to Virginia.

Blair hailed a taxi and relaxed into the seat.

"Where to, miss?"

"JFK, please," she answered and pulled out her cell to check for messages. She smiled when she saw the text from Tally wishing her luck for her presentation. Blair sent her a short note to let her know she'd call from the airport.

The driver wove through the hectic New York City traffic to bring Blair right to the departure gate. She paid the driver and tucked the receipt into her bag. Her small overnight case was waiting for her on the curb, and she retrieved it before walking into the terminal. The cold air welcomed her as she stepped inside and headed for the security gate. She tucked her sunglasses back into her bag and pulled out her ID. As a federal officer, she was allowed exclusive access through security where they checked her firearm and gave her a pass to the airline's VIP lounge to await the arrival of her flight. She smiled at the security team as she passed through the secured area and followed their directions to the room.

Blair located a comfortable recliner and settled in for her hour-long wait. She pulled out her cell and pressed the button to call Tally. The phone only rang twice before Tally answered.

"Hey, sweetie, I've got an hour wait until take-off, but I should be home by four. Be ready, and I'll help with the luggage, then we'll be on our way." She listened to Tally for several seconds. "Will you be okay in the storm?" she asked when Tally said a storm was about to move through. "Yes, I know you're all grown up, but that doesn't keep me from worrying. Love you, too, and I will see you soon."

Blair ended the call and felt the scowl on her face. Tally had been gifted with second sight when she was born with two different colored eyes. She had been teased during her childhood for being a freak by children and adults. It wasn't until she was nearly killed by a lightning strike at the age of twelve that she began to understand the gift that had been bestowed on her. Since that event, the proximity of an electrical storm frequently triggered her visions on numerous occasions. Blair was still a little spooked by Tally's psychic visions.

†

Tally tossed her cell on the bed and zipped up the last bag that she had packed for their trip. It had been months since she and Blair had been able to spend time away from work for some real relaxation, and she hoped it would be a few weeks before Blair was assigned to a new case. Most of their cases dealt with murder, the recovery of the victim, and the killer's discovery, but the last one they worked on together, a missing person case, turned out well. The missing teen was located, and they returned him home safely. The emotional trauma from the kidnapping would remain for his lifetime, but the teen could at least have the opportunity to live a long, healthy life.

Tally felt the hair on her arms standing up, and she knew the storm was close. Hopefully, it would move through quickly. She picked up her cell and took the last bag to the front foyer before entering the living room. Tally closed the blinds and sat on the couch to wait for the vision to come. She saw a flash of the lightning through the window, and she whispered to herself. "One, Mississippi, two Mississippi, three Mississippi, four Mississippi, boom." Tally had learned to count to gauge the storm's closeness from her mother when she was a child to help her deal with the anxiety she felt after the lightning strike. She closed her eyes and tucked her legs under her body to relax. Flash, boom, the storm had arrived, and her world went black.

Lisa, a young murder victim, had served as her spirit guide once Tally began to understand her visions. Lisa would help her communicate with the deceased, or help her visualize and locate the living, and help Tally use her gift to the fullest. Together they had allowed many victims of horrific crimes to be discovered and to cross over to a more peaceful existence. Today, however, Lisa had not appeared.

Tally felt like she was flying through a dense forest filled with thick green growths of trees. She could see birds and other small animals as she soared deeper into a dark canopied grove, and then suddenly, she was back in sunlight as the forest opened into a meadow. Tally was confused at first, as she saw gaping holes in the landscape, the dark soil mounded against the brilliant green grass. She sensed death on a large scale and scoured the ground for headstones that would indicate a cemetery or some form of a burial site. Finding none, Tally wondered if this were some sort of battlefield that once filled the grass with rivers of blood as warriors died in battle. Warriors seemed to be a strange thought, instead of soldiers, but that was the word that came to mind. Across the meadow, Tally saw a cluster of campers and tents, so she knew the vision was in the modern-day era. Smoke from a campfire wafted into the air as she searched for people. The site appeared abandoned until she caught a glimpse of a young woman kneeling by one of the mounds. She was bent over, slowly removing dirt from the ground with a small trowel. Tally strained to see what the young woman was trying to uncover, but she could not bring anything to view. She sensed sadness and death, but no other vision came to her. Just as quickly as she arrived at the scene, another flash of lightning sent her reeling back to her own reality.

Tally looked at her watch. Fifteen minutes had passed since she sat on the couch. The vision had left her unsettled. Usually, the purpose of the experience was apparent, but this one had been a teaser, and she wondered if there would be others to come that would give her more pieces to the puzzle she was being tasked to solve. She pondered where Lisa had been. It was unusual that she had not been present, even though that wasn't the first time Lisa had been absent.

"What is this all about?" Tally took out a notepad and jotted down the specifics of the vision. Tally had grown accustomed to doing this to keep facts straight and help her piece together the puzzle of images that appeared. When Tally finished, she reviewed her notes, but couldn't determine anything further.

"Only time will tell," Tally said. She closed her notepad and tucked it into her suitcase.

†

Blair watched the rain passing to the north as the jet came into land at the airport. *I hope the storm didn't upset Tally.* She knew how sensitive Tally was to the lightning associated with thunderstorms and how frequently her visions led to resolving a mysterious event. Selfishly, she hoped that if Tally had experienced a psychic episode, it would not interfere with their plans for a relaxing trip to the beach. They were both overdue for some respite from their stressful occupations. She glanced out the jet window, and when a flash of lightning filled the sky, she found herself counting, *one, Mississippi, two, Mississippi.* Blair smiled as she realized she was doing what she had witnessed Tally doing so many times. Calculating the distance from the storm.

Blair had followed in her dad's footsteps in the FBI and wasn't shy about using the assistance of psychics to help solve cases. Her dad had used a particular woman for years before he retired. When Blair first met Tally in Alabama, she was skeptical of the young woman's abilities, but her surprising accuracy was undeniable. As Tally gained the confidence of the task force hunting the serial killer, Blair found herself becoming attracted to Tally, and when she was kidnapped by the killer, Blair was fraught with guilt for letting her protective guard down. Even though she was just a few years older than Tally, her experience with the FBI had hardened her to the brutal nature of the crimes they investigated. Tally had a nurturing, naïve soul, and Blair felt destined to protect. Her feelings for Tally escalated quickly to a romantic attraction, and they became lovers and partners.

She looked at her watch. Home in forty-five minutes, then it would be sun and sand for four days.

The jet came to a stop on the tarmac. Blair quickly pulled her belongings together to exit the plane. Rushing through the terminal, she pulled out of the short-term parking before the rest of the passengers had time to collect their checked bags. *Just ten more minutes and I'll be home.* She pulled out her cell and called Tally.

"Hey baby, I'll be there in ten minutes." She could hear Tally chuckling. "Yeah, I know I'm overexcited, but I can't wait to have some uninterrupted time alone with you." She listened to Tally, who was equally excited. "You have the bags already at the front door? You must be ready, too. Okay, I'll see you soon. Love you."

The excitement in Tally's voice made her foot a little heavier on the gas pedal, and Blair made it in record time. When she bolted through the front door, she nearly knocked Tally over. She had been setting the thermostat on the air conditioning, and Blair's sudden appearance startled her. Blair laughed and took Tally in her arms.

"I know it was only one night away from you, but I missed you," she cried, and then kissed Tally.

When they ended the kiss, Tally grinned. "I missed you too. Grab those bags, and let's get going."

Blair wasted no time in picking up the two larger bags and racing out the door. Tally picked up the last bag and locked the door behind her before joining Blair at the car. She slipped into the passenger seat and pulled on a pair of sunglasses as Blair drove away.

"I'm sorry, I forgot to ask how you did in the storm. Is everything okay?"

Tally looked at Blair. "Everything's fine. A strange vision, but nothing we can't discuss when we get home."

"That sounds like a great plan to me."

"How long will it take us to get to the beach house?"

Blair flipped on the turn signal and smiled. "About two hours. I've already made arrangements to have groceries and other supplies delivered, so I thought we'd stop for an early dinner at one of the local spots and have a relaxing evening once we arrive."

"Sounds perfect to me." Tally slipped out of her shoes and stretched her legs out with her feet on the dash. "Vacation, here we come."

The whine of the tires and the warm sunshine coming through the windows lulled Tally into a nap. Blair turned the radio on and lowered the volume to keep from interrupting Tally's rest.

†

Blair slowed the car to exit the highway, and Tally's eyes opened.

"Sorry I crashed on you, but I didn't sleep well last night without you snuggling into me."

"I completely understand that. I missed snuggling with you, too. I need to gas up and use the restroom. Do you have any preferences for dinner?"

"I think we should take advantage of the fresh seafood while we're here."

"That sounds wonderful to me." Blair pulled into a service station and turned off the engine. "Would you mind pumping the gas while I go inside?" She offered Tally a credit card.

Tally smiled and took the card. "No problem. It's the least I can do for crashing on you."

"Thanks, sweetie," Blair answered and walked inside the store.

†

Tally climbed out of the car and walked to the pump. The sun was sinking on the horizon, and she could smell the ocean's salt in the air. She heard loud squawking and turned around to find three seagulls fighting over food scraps tossed out in the parking lot. Tally listened to the ocean waves in the distance, and chuckled at the angry birds, fighting over scraps when there was an ocean full of food waiting for them. "Lazy buggers," she said, and began pumping gas.

Blair finished in the restroom and was walking back through the store when something caught her eye. A rack of inexpensive souvenirs sat at the end of an aisle, and she chuckled when she saw keychains displaying the state slogan, *Virginia Beach is for lovers*. "It certainly is," she spoke to herself and bought a set of matching trinkets.

The clerk slipped her purchase into a small bag, and she returned outside to Tally, who was just finished filling the car.

"Do you want to go inside to wash your hands? The restroom is miraculously clean."

Tally grinned back at her. "Probably not a bad idea. I'll be right back."

Blair stowed her credit card and slipped behind the wheel. She placed the bag holding the key chains in Tally's seat and waited for her return.

†

In Huntsville, Texas, Casper Caruso sat on the bunk of his death row cell. The steam whistle had just blown for the midday prisoner count as he waited for his appointment. A guard came and gave him instructions to turn around and slide his hands through the slot to be cuffed for transport. Casper took his stack of papers to the door and pushed them through the slot. Then he turned around to slide his hands out the door. He felt the now-familiar chill of the steel cuffs as they slipped around his wrists and snapped closed with an audible click.

The guard signaled for the door to be unlocked and swung it open. "This is your big day, Caruso," he said with a grin. "Your last shot at appeals. I hope you've made it a good one."

Casper took the stack of papers from the guard. "One way or another, I plan to be leaving this wonderful abode. If the appeal for a new trial isn't granted, I'm going to request they move forward in scheduling my execution date. I'm sick of seeing these four walls."

"You should have thought about that years ago before you started killing. Did you really think you'd never get caught?"

Casper cackled an evil-sounding laugh. "I gave them a good run for a long time. Before they even knew the Ghost of East Texas existed."

"I think that was the beginning of your end. Thinking that you were smarter than law enforcement. If you hadn't started taunting them and stopped killing, you might not be standing here today."

"Maybe so." Casper nodded. "It wasn't like a light switch that I could turn on and off. After the first one, I just couldn't stop myself."

The guard huffed. "There will be a hot spot waiting for your arrival in hell for your actions."

"I'm sure I'll have plenty of company." Casper chuckled.

"No doubt about that," the guard said as he placed a hand on Caruso's shoulder to move him forward. "What number is this public defender? Five?"

"I've lost count of the losers they keep sending my way. It doesn't matter. I do all the legwork, and they just present the case." He shuffled along in front of the guard. "I probably could have done better representing myself from the beginning."

"As Honest Abe said, 'He who represents himself has a fool for a client.'"

"Yeah, I've heard that several times, but still, the clowns I get can barely seem to find a courtroom."

"Maybe you'll strike gold today."

"I ain't holding my breath. P. Herman is the lucky one today. I can only imagine what he's like."

"Well, that's going to be your first surprise," the guard teased. "P stands for Patricia."

"I'll be damned. Hopefully, she's a looker. The females around here aren't nothing to write home about."

"If you were a good-looking woman, would you want to work here with all this evil?"

"Good point. Still, it would be nice to see a real looker for a change."

Caruso smiled as the guard opened the door to the small conference area, and a beautiful, red-haired woman sat waiting at the table.

"Well, I'll be damned, wishes do come true," he whispered to the guard.

"Good morning, Mr. Caruso. I'm Patricia Herman. I've been assigned counsel for your last round of appeals."

"Good morning to you, too."

The guard took the stack of papers from him, placed them on the table, then unlocked one side of his handcuffs, and secured it on the massive metal ring. Caruso took his seat and reached for his stack of papers on the table in front of him.

"Is that really necessary?" the lawyer asked as the guard secured the cuff to the table.

"Trust me, it's necessary and facility policy. I'll be outside if you need anything," the guard said, and stepped outside the door to give the two privacy.

"Thank you, officer," the woman answered.

When she turned back to Caruso, she changed her smile to a more serious face. "I won't lead you on with a great deal of hope. I've read your entire case file, and it wasn't pretty. This is your final chance for an appeal. If this doesn't work, I can send a proposal to the judge to commute your sentence to life."

Casper shook his head. "I'd rather stay on death row than to be released to that jungle of insanity. If the appeal is not successful, I want you to request an execution date be set. I'd rather be dead than spend more time rotting in this hell."

"If that's what you really wish," she said as she reached for the papers.

"It is, no doubt."

"Well, let's see what you have prepared."

Caruso watched the woman read through page after page of his final written appeal.

"It's too bad, you didn't go to school. You could have made a great legal aide. You did some excellent research on this."

"Ha! Legal aides make what, thirty thousand a year? I was making three times that on the oil rigs."

"Then why blow it all for a life of crime and imprisonment?"

Caruso leaned forward across the table. "Because, pretty lady, taking someone's life gave me more pleasure than even the best sex could have ever accomplished. After the first one, I became addicted to it, and I needed more and more."

Her recoil was visible. "You have no remorse for what you did to those six women?"

"None at all for them, or the others." Caruso smiled at the look of surprise that crossed the lawyers face. "Yes, there were more than six, but the FBI could only prove six. They might never know about the others."

"I think we need to end this line of conversation here," she said. "I'll be back in touch. Are you one hundred percent sure about your decision to move forward with execution if this fails?"

"Absolutely. Have a great day," he said as she picked up his paperwork and left the room quickly.

The guard opened the door. "That was quick. I thought you might have drawn this out for hours."

Caruso stood and stretched. "No need to waste time on a lost cause."

"Probably not," the guard said, snapping the cuff closed behind his back. "Well, let's get you back home."

They walked back to the cell he had lived in for the last ten years, and after being released from the cuffs, Caruso sat at the small desk and started writing a letter.

CHAPTER TWO

"Oh, my goodness, I can't eat another bite," Tally declared as she pushed her plate away.

Blair reached over to take the last shrimp from her plate. "I guess that means I'm all alone in eating dessert."

"Dessert? I forgot about the key lime pie on the menu." Tally frowned.

Blair smiled at her lover. "It's still early. Let's get a coffee and let dinner settle, and then you may want that pie. Or if you'd prefer, we can get a pie to take with us."

"Let's do that. We can unload our bags at the beach house. That will give us an appetite for pie."

When the waiter returned, Blair ordered a pie to go and paid the check. Darkness was falling around them when they exited the restaurant and walked to the car.

"After we get settled in, why don't we take a walk on the beach. There's supposed to be a full moon tonight, Blair suggested."

"That sounds perfect. I'm ready for some sand between my toes."

†

When they arrived at the beach, they carried their bags inside.

"I'll put these away if you'll make us a coffee and serve the pie."

"A big slice for both of us?" Blair asked.

"Yes, darling, we can walk those calories off on the beach."

"Or later, when we get back." Blair wiggled her eyebrows and chuckled.

"We may need seconds on the pie then," Tally said as she took the first bag to the bedroom to unpack.

"I'm glad we bought a whole pie now," Blair called after her. "We may need it."

"I can guarantee, not a crumb of it will go to waste," Tally called back to her.

"I do like the sound of that," Blair said to herself as she opened cabinets looking for supplies. She cut two large slices of pie and placed the rest in the fridge as she waited for the coffee to brew, then took the last two bags to the large

16

bedroom overlooking the beach. She opened the curtains and door to let the early evening sea breeze into the room.

"We've waited too long to return here. My soul feels much better already."

Tally walked up and hugged her from behind as they started out at the water. "We both need a good cleansing. It's been a rough few month, hasn't it?"

"It has been hectic. Unfortunately, evil never rests."

"That is all too true. All these mass murders and young people dying for no reason has weighed down our souls. Hopefully, a few days here will do us both some good."

Blair turned in Tally's arms and kissed her. "I love how you always remain so positive. Your energy and love are just what I needed in my life."

"Fate brought us together, and our love will only continue to grow."

"Yes, it will. You want to set up the bathroom while I finished unpacking these bags?"

"Sure, baby. Our coffee sounds like it's ready and the pie is cut."

"I should be finished when you get done with the hygiene supplies. I love you."

"Love you more," Blair said before planting another soft kiss on Tally's lips and walking to the bathroom with the small bag in tow.

Tally smiled and turned at a flicker of heat lightning that flashed in the distance across the water. She was glad it did not have the same effect as lightning in a thunderstorm and resumed her unpacking.

When finished, they enjoyed the pie and coffee before stepping out onto the deck. Both were eager for a walk to the beach. Blair and Tally kicked off their shoes and were about to step onto the boardwalk when Blair, stopped. "Hang on a sec," she said and walked into the house and returned carrying a flashlight. "You never know," she grinned and took Tally's hand to walk to the shore.

They walked for a half-hour before turning back toward the house. The moon had started to rise as they returned. There was a soft breeze blowing in their faces, just stiff enough to blow the hair from Tally's face.

"I've been blessed with a beautiful night and even more precious company," Blair said. "Are you ready to head inside?"

"Yes, if you are," Tally answered.

"I'm ready for a nice shower and a relaxing evening with you."

"That sounds perfect to me. It's so peaceful here, we lose all track of time."

Blair looked at her watch as they stepped onto the deck. "Wow, you aren't kidding, it's already ten."

"I hope the rest of our time doesn't go by this fast."

"Hopefully, it won't, but it will never be enough time with you." Blair opened the door, and they stepped inside. "There's one other thing I need to do." Blair picked up her cell phone from the table and turned it off. "There, now we will have a total escape from the world for a few days."

"What if your dad calls?"

"He won't, but if he doesn't reach my cell and it's an emergency, he'll call the house and leave a message."

Blair walked back to the door to make sure it was locked. "Are you ready to shower?"

"Just waiting for you." Tally reached out her hand.

18

Clothing hit the floor as they made their way to the shower. The warm water and tender caresses had them both relaxed and refreshed for an evening of slow, gentle lovemaking.

Afterward, Tally snuggled into Blair. "I'm not sure if I enjoy our lovemaking or the snuggle time with you more."

"I'll take them both. It seems like we get so little time together without the weight of the world on our shoulders. If I ever forget to tell you enough, know that I love you with every ounce of me."

"That is always enough for me. Goodnight, my love," Tally answered with a dreamy quality in her voice.

Blair reached over to turn out the light and pulled the covers over their bodies. The breeze was gentle as it brought the ocean's fresh scent into the room, and the crashing of the waves drew her into slumber.

†

The tapping of rain on the metal roof woke Blair the next morning, and she crept from the bed to close the window. The weatherman had predicted light showers for the early morning, then the rest of their vacation should be bathed in the sun. Tally was curled up on her side, one bare leg poking out from the covers, still sleeping soundly as Blair left the room. She closed the door gently behind her and walked to the kitchen to prepare coffee and breakfast.

She had fresh melon sliced, eggs, bacon, toast, and coffee prepared, and was placing it on the serving table when the door cracked open, and Tally stuck her head in.

19

"Oh, no, you don't. Back to bed with you. I'm serving breakfast in bed to you this morning."

"Yes, my love," Tally answered and walked back to the bed.

Blair set the tray in front of her and leaned down for a morning kiss.

"This looks delicious. Will you be joining me?"

"Yes, love, I'll be right back."

Blair returned a few moments later with her own tray of food. She sat next to Tally on the bed. "The rain woke me, so I thought I'd make us breakfast."

"It's raining?" Tally looked disappointed.

"Not anymore. It's moved through quickly, and it promises to be beautiful for the rest of our stay."

Tally's smile lit the room. "That's great news. What are we doing today?"

"Playing tourist. I've got us booked for a whale watching tour at two. I've heard from a good authority that seeing whales right now is highly probable."

"Even if we don't, I'm sure we will see dolphins and other ocean life." Tally was excited about the new adventure.

"After we finish breakfast, we can shower, dress for the day, and head to town to wander through some of the seaside shops, if you'd like. I also need to stop by a pharmacy."

"Are you not feeling well?" Tally asked with a frown.

"I'm fine, sweetheart. You've never been out on the ocean, so I wanted to get us some motion sickness patches, just as a precaution. The water can get rough at times."

"Oh, I hadn't given thought to that. Better safe than sorry, I guess. I don't want to hurl over the side of the boat, and I'm sure you don't need to experience that either."

Blair shook her head. "Not at all how I want you to spend your first trip out to sea. We won't be going very far out, but I'm not willing to risk you getting ill. Me either for that matter. I've never been seasick, but there's always a first."

"This breakfast is too good to lose. Thank you for such a wonderful surprise."

"My pleasure, sweetheart. We can grab an early lunch in town before we get on the boat. I hear there's a true New York pizza place that's opened since we were here last."

"That sounds yummy, but maybe not the best thing to eat before going out to sea. Can we have something lighter, and I'll treat us to pizza after we survive the boat trip?"

Blair grinned at Tally. "You do make a good point. Maybe just a sandwich then."

†

After they finished breakfast, Blair put her camera battery on charge and helped Tally clean the kitchen. "I swear I didn't mean to make this big of a mess," she said as she dumped the melon rinds into the garbage.

"That breakfast was wonderful. Besides, I'm usually the one who dirties up every dish in the kitchen when I cook."

"True, but you've also mastered cleaning as you cook," Blair said, and stopped long enough to give Tally a quick peck to her cheek as she removed the garbage bag to take it outside.

Tally chuckled. "You do have a point there. You're still a work in progress."

She waited until Blair returned. "What do you suggest we wear today? Will it be cooler out on the water?"

"Probably so. I'd suggest jeans and a T-shirt. We can also take a light jacket in case we get chilled."

†

Haley Salem, a Mississippi State archeology student, had been bent over the same pit for several hours. She stood and stretched the muscles in her back and legs. She looked across to the campsite, filled with tents, campers, and a few small motorhomes, but she was the sole survivor of the dig site. It was a long four-day school break, and the others in her group had decided to take a respite from the dig to spend the long, holiday weekend partying in nearby New Orleans. Even her girlfriend, Beth, still in Starkville in nursing school, had suggested she take a break, but Haley felt like she was onto something big. They had worked the dig site just off the Natchez Trace for weeks and had found pottery shards and a few Civil War era items, but something had drawn her to this particular spot, and she had a gut feeling she would uncover something extraordinary. Beth had promised to drive down the following day, so Haley wanted to put as much energy as she could into the site. Once Beth arrived, they could have some private time alone in her camper. There was no way Beth was about to sleep in a tent, so Haley had borrowed a small camper from her uncle. She had not regretted the decision when the frequent thunderstorms arrived, and she had shelter over her head, while the more die-hard macho men on the crew dug trenches around their tents, but still ended up getting soaked.

†

The sun had returned from behind the bank of clouds that had hidden it earlier, and several rays were beating down on the pit. A bright object was peeking through the dark dirt where Haley had dug all morning. She leaned down to get a better look, and her eyes flew open when she saw bone gleaming back up at her. "I knew it," she cried out as loud as she could, and several crows returned her scream and flew off in the distance. Her heart was pumping wildly as she grabbed her trowel and brush and knelt back inside the pit. She carefully removed the loosened dirt to reveal a handle of some sort, and as she continued to brush, the mud-encrusted blade of a knife came into view. The knife was crossed with another blade, that she thought was strange, but she carefully moved dirt until a second handle and blade were revealed. She could see carvings in the handles, but could not make them out from a distance. She sat back on her heels and took a deep breath.

†

Haley raced back to the camper to retrieve her camera. She remembered how important it was to document each step of a significant find for evidence, and she was sure she had uncovered something remarkable.

She took photographs from various angles to document the location of the objects in the dig site and then placed her camera on the tarp. When she leaned forward, her fingers trembled with excitement as she carefully reached for the first handle and cautiously lifted it from its resting place.

23

Haley examined it briefly and lowered it onto a burlap sack she had folded up sitting beside her. When she returned for the second knife, the ground had a much firmer grip on it, and she used the tip of the trowel to slowly pull the dirt from around the object. When the handle pulled free of the soil, she lifted it out of the pit and laid it beside its mate.

"Mate? That's a strange word to have thought of, but it seems to fit, and it popped into my head." She picked up her camera and took several more photographs of the knives now resting on the burlap.

†

Haley climbed from the pit and placed the tarp over the dig site. She wanted to take her finds to the covered area to see if she could clean them enough to recognize the carvings' details on the handles. Haley picked up the burlap sack and carried her precious cargo across the open field. The large barn owl that had sat perched on a limb on a dying old oak for days watched her as she crossed the clearing. He swooped down to the ground and grabbed a field mouse in his talons, before taking flight and landing back in the tree.

"Someone has his dinner," she said as she passed by him, and his beak tore at the dead rodent. Her own stomach growled in protest, reminding her the last thing she had eaten was the granola bar she gobbled down before starting to work, eight hours earlier. "Food will have to wait for now. I only have so much daylight left."

†

She laid the burlap, and her camera on a bare table, then gathered several small tools and a pan of clean water. She pulled a water bottle from the cooler and took a long drink before pulling a wooden stool up to the table. Haley picked up the first knife and gently dipped it into the pan of water to loosen the mud caked to it, moving it slowly through the water. The water turned dark as the fertile soil separated from the metal and bone. The blade from the knife remained dull from age and countless years of being buried, but it appeared to be solidly made. She was tempted to remove some of the rust, but she resisted her urge to be careless, took the knife from the water, and picked up a soft cloth to pat away the water. Haley turned the handle in her hands, examining the carving in the bone. Both sides of the handle were carved almost identically. In the broadest section of the handle was an engraving of the sun, and beneath it, a native warrior wearing what appeared to be a feathered headdress knelt down in reverence. Someone had taken great care to carve the handle so perfectly. She rolled it gently in her hands, marveling at the beauty of the art.

†

Eager to uncover the carvings on the other knife, she carefully placed the first cleaned knife in the soft cloth. She dumped out the pan of water and poured in several inches of clean water. She repeated the process she had used with the other knife, and as the soil loosened from the bone, a beautiful carving ran the handle's length. A warrior's body was covered with a giant snake, or serpent, from his foot to

25

his mouth, carved into the bone. The shape of the serpent had designs, like tattoos over its body. Suns were prominent, but once more Native American warriors were also present, along with horses and other animals. It was a work of art that had taken long hours of tedious work to create.

She rolled the knife in her hands and saw the same carving on the other side of the handle. Haley retrieved her camera and took pictures of both of the objects. Darkness was quickly falling, and a cool breeze had begun to blow as she sat mesmerized by the beauty of her find. The barn owl hooted from his perch, breaking the near silence of the falling night, startling Haley out of a trance. After carefully wrapping each knife in a clean, soft cloth, Haley carried them into her camper and placed them on the small dining room table.

†

Haley entered the bathroom and washed her hands before returning to the kitchen to prepare a sandwich and salad for her dinner. She sat down to eat and placed her phone on the table. She checked for messages and then turned on her hot spot, hoping for a strong enough signal to use her laptop for some research. Luck was with her. She had a secure connection and pushed her dinner away and placed her laptop on the table. She turned it on and quickly accessed the internet. She typed in several keywords and pulled up a file on the Natchez Native Americans. She downloaded the file and keyed in several other search keywords to pull up additional data. She was in the process of downloading when her signal failed.

"Shit," she yelled as the signal died, and the download could not complete. "At least I got some stuff downloaded." Haley opened the file and started to read.

†

"If you're ready, let's head back to the car to drop these bags off. Then we can go ahead and drive to the harbor for our trip." Blair reached for the package of Dramamine patches and read the instructions. She removed one, placed the round dot behind Tally's right ear, and repeated the same actions for herself. "All set," she said as they left the pharmacy and walked to the car.

It was a short drive to the harbor, and it didn't take long for them to reach the boat they would be going out on. Blair grabbed her camera from the back seat and took Tally's hand as they walked to the whale excursion boat's mooring spot.

"Stand there for just a second and let me get a shot of you," Blair said and motioned to a place for Tally to pose. When she had taken several photos, a man walked up beside her.

†

"Would you like to have one with both of you?"

"Yes, thanks, that would be terrific." Blair handed him the camera and smiled when she recognized the captain of the ship. "Good to see you again, Jim."

"Likewise, Blair. It's been a long time. How's the old man?"

"Enjoying the hell out of retirement. I hope we all make it there one day."

"Patience, young one, don't wish your life away," he teased.

"I plan on taking every advantage life has to offer. I hear we have a good chance of seeing some whales today."

"Yes, ma'am, we've been fortunate for a few days." He waved her off to stand beside Tally. "All set, ladies?"

"Whenever you are," Blair called back and placed an arm around Tally.

Jim took several photographs of the couple and took a step toward them. "Take a look and make sure I didn't cut off any heads." He chuckled as he handed Blair her camera. He took an appraising look at Tally. "You must be Tally Rainwater," he said and offered her his hand. "Jim Stone."

"Captain Jim Stone," Blair interjected.

"Captain, owner, chief cook and bottle washer of this here vessel, at your service ma'am," he said with a bow.

"Very nice to meet you, sir," Tally said with a laugh.

"Oh, a southern belle. I just love the accent."

"What accent?" Tally asked with a wink.

"North Georgia, if I had to wager a guess."

"Damn, you have always been good at that," Blair teased. She turned to Tally and nodded her head toward Jim. "The good captain here retired from the bureau not long before my dad."

"I've been following your career, and you ladies make one heck of a team. You've done some excellent work together."

"We have, indeed, and we're here for some rest and relaxation, so no more shop talk."

"I understand completely. Come on board and let me show you around the old gal. She ain't the prettiest in the harbor, but the boat is solid and reliable."

"Where's the best spot for a viewing?"

"Right up front, Blair. Only one other couple is joining the tour today, so you'll have pretty much free roam on deck. If you get cold or need a break, feel free to join me in the wheelhouse. I've got a fresh pot of coffee if you're interested."

Tally smiled up at him, "That does sound good."

"Follow me then, little missy." He grinned and led them into the wheelhouse for coffee while they waited for the other passengers to arrive.

"Has business been slow?"

"Are you kidding? Today is the first day I haven't been packed to the rails with guests. I'm glad you have a semi-private tour, though, to share the experience."

"This is Tally's virgin voyage out to sea," Blair said. "We took precautions, just in case," she added as she pointed to the little white dot behind her ear.

"Better safe than sorry. The water should be calm for our trip, but I think there's a storm brewing later."

"Damn that weatherman. He predicted sunshine for the rest of the weekend," Blair groaned.

"I'm okay with it, as long as it comes at night, and I'm not out on the water. It's been a weird weather season all around," he added.

"Yeah, it has," Blair agreed.

"Here comes our other couple. You guys want to take up the front position? I'll keep them in the back."

"Like you said, we've pretty much got the whole boat to ourselves, so we can make room in the front if they want to join us." Blair smiled at him. "You want me to cast you off?"

"Naw, Danny, from the next boat over, will be out in just a second to cast us off. Thanks for asking, though."

"Not a problem." Blair took Tally's hand and led her to the front of the boat to a small bench. "You want to sit for a few?"

"Sure," Tally answered. "It's such a beautiful day."

"I hope the weatherman is wrong again."

"No worries, especially if it's later this evening. We can light a fire in the fireplace and cuddle on the couch."

Blair smiled. "Since you put it that way, bring on the rain." She picked up her camera and walked to the railing before turning around to catch Tally gazing at the other boats in the harbor. *She's so beautiful.* Tally turned toward her and smiled, just as Blair took another shot.

"That one's definitely a keeper," Blair said as she looked into the viewfinder at the picture she had just snapped.

†

Haley heard the rumble of thunder in the distance and grabbed a flashlight before heading outside. She wanted to make sure the tarp over her dig site was secure in case it rained She didn't cherish the thought of toiling through the mud to continue her search. The hoot of the owl sent a chill down her spine. Even though she had seen him nearly every day for weeks, the sound made the eerie night a little spookier.

"Come on, Haley, just because you're alone, don't go spooking yourself out." Even her voice sounded strange in the dark night. The full moon had risen and cast a pathway to her site as she rushed across the meadow. The temperature had dropped noticeably, and Haley could feel the moisture in the air. She located several large stones that she used to anchor her tarp, to seal the area from the impending rain. Haley placed the last stone just as a blood-curdling scream came from deep in the forest. The cry was followed by excited yips and a loud growl as coyotes hunted their prey. Haley knew the hunt was a great distance away, but she wasted no time returning to her camper's safety. She opened a drawer by the bed and pulled out her handgun.

"Better safe than sorry," she whispered to herself and locked the door.

When her heart rate settled, she sat at the table and resumed reading the file she had opened. Haley knew the area had been a Natchez tribe settlement in the 1700s, and it was near what was now known as the Emerald Mound just south of Stanton, Mississippi. As she read, she discovered that the paramount Chief of the Tribe was called the Great Sun, and his younger brother, the war chief, was called the Tattooed Serpent, who had died in 1725.

Suddenly, the carvings on the knife handle made perfect sense to her. Haley wondered if she had uncovered the burial sites of these two prominent leaders. She was confused, though, why they would be buried here instead of at the Emerald Mound. She crossed her fingers and tried to connect to the internet once more.

†

Blair was overjoyed with Tally's laughter as dolphins swam beside the boat, breaching and performing acrobatics just for her. Her lens was torn between the joy on Tally's face and the antics on the water. Jim had been correct and had provided them with a beautiful afternoon. They were able to follow a pod of whales for nearly an hour before they reached a point they had to turn around. The pod swam close to the boat, and they caught glimpses of a young whale, ushered to the center of the group by a protective mother.

When Jim turned the boat back toward the harbor, he raced a bank of clouds to the shore. The winds had picked up as the temperature dropped significantly, and Tally balked at first about going inside for shelter from the wind, but a massive wave crashing against the bow convinced her it was time. She took Blair's hand and was laughing as they entered the wheelhouse.

"I was about ready to come to retrieve you two. It's going to be a bit rough as we head in. There's fresh coffee if you want a cup. Have a seat, and I'll get us back as soon as I can."

"Thanks, Jim. It's been a great afternoon. Everything you promised and more." Tally surprised Blair by hugging his neck.

"Well, I'm glad you've had a great time. How's your stomach?"

"I'm feeling great," she replied, and then took the coffee Blair handed her.

Blair grinned at her, "Good enough to try out the new pizza place for dinner?"

"If you're talking about the new spot on Main, it's awesome. I've not gotten anything from there that wasn't great," Jim told them.

"Can we get one to take home?"

"I don't see why not," Blair answered. "That gets me out of cooking tonight."

"We're supposed to be on vacation," Tally reminded her.

"I know. Trust me, I don't mind one bit," Blair said with a wink to Jim.

"Sounds like you've got the night all settled. Try to beat this weather. It looks like it's not that far behind us," he warned. "I've got the number programmed into my phone if you want to call and order in."

Blair nodded, "That would be smart. How long until we get back to the harbor?"

"About thirty minutes," he answered after looking at his watch.

"Can I get anything for you?" Blair asked as she plugged the number into her phone?

"Thanks, but tonight is date night. I've been roped into dinner and a movie with Jill."

"Tell her hello for me. I know you'll have a great time."

He chuckled. "As long as Jill doesn't pick a chick flick."

Blair bumped him with her shoulder. "You know you love em, but you won't admit it."

He grinned and shrugged. "I do up to the point they make me cry," he admitted.

"You're just a big ole teddy bear, Jim," Blair teased.

"Shush now, you're going to ruin my rep," he answered.

Tally grinned. "Your secret is safe with me."

†

Casper crumpled up the paper and tossed it into the trash with his three previous attempts. He pulled out a fresh piece of paper.

Dear Special Agent Cooper,

I know I'm the last person you expected to get a letter from, but I need to say things to you. Something that can only be shared in a face-to-face meeting. I'd recommend you bring that psychic freak with you. You're going to need her help. My time is drawing near, so don't wait long to make a decision. I've decided to give you what you were unable to uncover for yourself. I'm sure several families would appreciate your effort.

With all respect.

The Ghost of East Texas

Casper smiled at his clever little note that was sure to bait the FBI agent into a Texas trip. He would get his last fifteen minutes of fame and leave this world on top of his game. He folded the note and placed it in his Bible. He was almost assured that his final appeal would be denied, and an execution date would be filed within the next few weeks. Once he learned his eventual fate, the last duty of P. Herman, Public Defender, would be to invite Cooper for a meeting. That was the least she could do after failing to obtain approval for an appeal. He grinned as he closed the Bible and listened to the final whistle of the day.

"All accounted for," he said. "Not even close," he chuckled and walked over to his cot.

He stretched out on the cot and stared out the tiny window of his cell. The dark night sky was lit up by distant lightning and he closed his eyes, waiting for the storm.

CHAPTER THREE

Blair grabbed the pizza box, and they made a dash for the door just as the first raindrops began to fall.

"We cut that pretty close." She opened the door and turned to Tally. "If you'll get us some plates and a drink, I'll start the fireplace."

"Would you like a beer with our pizza?"

"You must have been reading my mind," Blair said, and then reached behind Tally's ear to peel off her patch. "I think we can lose these now."

Tally smiled. "I had forgotten all about the patch. That was a brilliant idea, by the way."

"Thank you, my dear," Blair answered as she placed the box on the coffee table, walked to the fireplace, took out a long match, and opened the flue. She heard the winds picking up outside, swirling around the house as she watched the flames begin to lick the kindling as the fire came to life. Blair listened to the wood crackling, and hoped if the storm had been brought in lightning, it would hold off until later in the night.

Tally returned from the kitchen with plates, napkins, and two beers. Blair flipped the lid open on the box.

"Man, that smells good," she said as Tally handed her a plate.

"Couch or fireplace?" Tally asked.

"Let's toss some pillows down and sit by the fire. It's going to be toasty soon."

"Now you're reading my mind." Tally chuckled and tossed several large pillows in front of the fireplace. "That should do it," she said as she wiped her hands together. "Let's eat."

"Did you work up an appetite today, love?" Blair handed her a plate with several slices of the pizza.

"I think it was all the fresh air. The smell from that pizza box on the ride home was excruciating, as well. My stomach has been growling like a ravenous beast."

"A ravenous beast, huh? Well, let's feed that beast of yours." Blair picked up her plate and the beers, before taking a seat beside her lover.

†

Haley nearly shouted when her internet suddenly connected after an irritatingly long five minutes of waiting. Her fingers flew across the keyboard as she frantically downloaded several documents on the history of the Natchez Tribe, specifically the tribes in Mississippi and Louisiana. She was seconds away from finishing the download of a large file when the connection started to fade. "Come on, hold out for just a few more seconds…got it!"

She went to her hard drive and opened the first of the downloaded files. Her eyes flew to diagrams of the icons worshipped by the tribes. First, the sun, and she read that the Great Sun was the prominent chieftain, adorned with a brilliantly feathered headdress, and a loincloth with a radiant sun woven into the material. Haley surmised that his broad jaw and charming smile accentuated his charismatic allure to his followers. He was surrounded by children, evidence of his virility, reportedly birthed by several mothers. The children were beautiful, and they looked up at the Chief with adoration. The next image was of the Tattooed Serpent, the brother of the Chief, and the War Chief of the tribe. His chiseled features and wizened face made it easy to visualize young warriors following him into battle, to their deaths if necessary, for their nation's glory.

The third image, a flying creature, similar in features to a dragon, was called the Piasa Bird. The colorful scales accentuated the beast's beauty, while the human and cat-like face was surrounded by fierce antlers and large talons. The bird had a long, whip-like tail that wound around his entire body. The passage described the mural of the Piasa on cliff walls along the Mississippi River in what is now Alton, Illinois, and the urban legend that sprang from the first recorded sighting by explorer Father Jacques Marquette on his journey down the Mississippi River. The Piasa Bird was told to attack villages and could carry off a warrior in its massive talons. The legend described how a local chief, Chief Ouatoga, had a dream where the Great Spirit shared how to kill the gigantic creature. Ouatoga called out twenty of his bravest warriors and armed them with poisoned arrows, and then the chief himself acted as bait to lure the monster from its cave. The story tells that the mural was painted when the creature was killed, while others claimed it was a warning to travelers that they were entering into Cahokia territory.

"Wow, this is definitely going on my bucket list," Haley said aloud.

Haley picked up a pen to make some notes when the lights in the camper flickered. In the excitement of the day, she had forgotten to refuel the generator. Cursing herself, Haley grabbed a flashlight and left the camper. The winds had picked up, and she heard the faint rumbling of thunder in the distance. The moon had fully risen, and Haley could see the glow coming off the barn owl's feathers as it continued its stoic surveillance. She quickly refilled the tank on the generator and started it again, then made her way to the front of the camper. Haley felt the hairs on the back of her neck raise like hackles, and turned back toward the open meadow. She thought she was being watched, and a cold shiver ran down her spine. Haley rushed inside the camper and locked the door behind her. She wasn't someone who became rattled quickly, but something had her on edge.

She returned to the table but found it impossible to focus, so she changed into sleepwear and crawled between her covers. She placed her pistol on the small bedside table and turned off the lamp. The rain began to tap, tap, tap on the camper's metal roof, and she felt her eyes grow heavy.

†

They had finished eating, and Blair noticed Tally had become silent. "The storm is coming, isn't it?"

Tally nodded. "I feel it's close. The hair on my arms is standing straight up." She held out her arm so Blair could see the hair standing at attention.

"Do you want to get on the couch or the bed to be more comfortable?"

"I think I'll go into the bedroom if that's okay."

Blair smiled. "Of course, it is. I'll be right here waiting on you," she said, pointing to the comfortable pile of pillows. She kissed Tally. "I was hoping you'd have some peace, but some things are out of our control."

"It's okay," Tally answered. "I'll be back soon."

Blair watched her lover leave the room and then went to the counter to retrieve her camera. She piled up on the pillows and began to scroll through the photographs she had taken. The smile on Tally's face in the photos warmed her heart.

†

Tally walked into the bedroom just as the first clap of thunder arrived. She knew that her visions unsettled Blair, so she had left the room to relax in comfort. Tally kicked off her shoes and climbed onto the bed, placing pillows behind her back. She closed her eyes and searched the darkness for Lisa. There was no need to count. The storm had moved quickly

40

and was in full force as the winds and rain battered the beach house.

The vision that appeared before her was anything but her treasured spirit guide. Instead, she saw two young Native American girls, and she guessed them to be in their early teen years, naked from the waist up, wearing only long skirts that reached mid-shin. They were beautiful, and Tally saw love in their eyes as they looked at one another, and leaned forward to join their lips in a soft kiss. Then they joined hands and walked across a verdant meadow and disappeared in a mist.

Tally's vision shifted, and she was looking through another's eyes. The person she assumed was a woman, based on the delicate hands that caressed a knife with a bone handle. The woman examined the carving of a warrior in the grip. A serpent was wrapped around his body from his feet to his neck. The artwork was gorgeous, and Tally got the impression it was a ceremonial knife, or at least a prized possession. She had no further clue how the blade and the girls and the woman she had seen before were connected, but she felt something important that she would piece together.

Oddly, her vision shifted again, and she was inside a small room, starkly decorated, and she realized it was a prison cell. Stretched out on the bed was a handsome blond man, his feet propped on the end of his cot as he appeared to be dreaming. She recognized the clothing as a prison jumpsuit, but she had no further clue to his identity. She had never seen him before, and it surprised her that his image followed so closely the two visions she was sure were connected. Just as quickly as the vision arrived, Tally found herself wandering through the darkness until she found her way back to the bedroom. She opened her eyes and reached for her notepad and began writing furiously.

†

Blair, concerned about the length of time Tally had been gone, walked to the bedroom to check on her. The storm had moved through as quickly as it had arrived. She found Tally sitting on the edge of the bed, writing in her notebook. Tally was so engrossed in her writing that she failed to hear Blair's approach. Knowing that Tally was writing down the details of her vision, Blair quietly turned away and walked back to the fire. She snuggled back into the pile of pillows and waited for her lover to return.

When Blair saw Tally enter the room, she immediately noticed the scowl on her face. "Are you okay?"

"Yes, why do you ask?"

"Because of that scowl you're wearing. Is it from your vision?"

"Probably, but I'm not sure of which one. I had three this time, and it's frustrating trying to connect how the three are connected."

"Are you ready to talk about them?"

"No, but maybe you can help me make sense of them. Let me grab my notepad."

Blair sat up next to the pile of pillows, and when Tally returned, she sat next to Blair with her legs crossed Indian style and flipped open her notepad.

Thirty minutes later, when Tally finished reading her notes, Blair scratched her head. "I'll be honest, I'm not quite sure what to make of your visions. I'm sorry I can't be of help."

Tally sighed and placed her notepad on the table. "It's not your fault. We just don't have enough information to piece it all together yet. Lisa's absence in these visions also has me confused. Just when I need her the most, she's gone AWOL."

Blair chuckled. "That seems such a weird thing to say about a spirit guide. It's hardly like she's gone on vacation. You don't think she's finally crossed over, do you?"

Tally's eyes grew wide at Blair's comment. "Not without telling me what she was doing, but her absence certainly leaves me confused. Do you think it's because, in at least two of the visions, the people in them still appear alive?"

"Sweetheart, I think I'm the last person who could give you advice on that. It does seem really odd, her absence, I mean. Lisa is usually there to help you."

Blair stretched her legs out in front of her and laid back against the large pillows. She smiled when Tally placed her notepad on the coffee table and stretched out next to her. Blair wrapped a protective arm around her lover and held her close. "Don't worry. We will get to the bottom of these visions. We always have, and we will continue to work through them. I reckon when it's time for us to know how they are connected, we're clever enough to figure it out."

"I know you're right, Blair, but I'll be worried until I know more."

"I'd be worried about you if you didn't worry." She chuckled. "Boy, say that five times fast."

"No, thank you. I think I'd rather just snuggle in with you and enjoy this nice fire you have built for us."

"Pretty damn good if I say so myself," Blair answered as her fingers played in Tally's hair.

†

Casper felt the hair on his arms stand at attention and felt a strange chill pass through him. The cell had grown dark. Only the sliver of light that crept through the window from the full moon illuminated the small area. His eyes searched the small space, but he was alone in his cell. He couldn't shake the feeling of being watched, and he tried to close his eyes to will sleep to take him, but the eerie feeling remained.

"Shit." He spoke aloud and sat up on his bunk. He walked to his small table area and turned on the lamp, but he still felt the presence in the dark shadows. "I must be finally losing my mind."

His eyes fell on the small notepad by the lamp, and he picked up his pencil and started to make a list. He had no idea why he was compelled to make a list, but he felt more at ease once it was finished. He read over the list of items and put down his pencil.

"This should do just fine." Content that he had completed the task he was compelled to complete, Casper turned off the lamp and returned to his bunk. The heaviness in the shadows was still present, but he closed his eyes and drifted off to sleep

†

Blair smiled as she felt Tally relax in her arms. She knew that the visions Tally experienced frequently left her physically and emotionally drained. She held her lover close until the fire burned down and then gently shook her awake.

"Baby, let's call it a night and head to bed."

Tally jolted awake despite Blair's attempts to be gentle. "Dammit, I did it again, didn't I? I fell asleep on you."

"You did, but I don't mind. I know what your visions take out of you. Besides, I rather enjoyed holding you close and watching the fire."

Tally ran her hand through her hair. "How long did I sleep?"

"Not that long. I'm sure all the fresh air we had today added to your need for sleep. I was starting to nod off myself, so I thought it was time to hit the sheets."

"I'm sorry."

Blair brushed the hair from Tally's face. "I'm not. This time is for us to relax, nothing more." She offered Tally her hand. "We have all weekend, so tonight, let's rest. Tomorrow is a new day." She turned toward Tally and raised the shirt above her head. "Nightclothes?" she asked.

"No, I want to feel your skin next to mine."

"Great answer," Blair said and stepped forward to kiss her lover.

"More."

"More what?"

"More of those," Tally replied and slipped out of her pants.

Blair cocked her head. "Second wind?"

"Power nap." Tally slipped her hand under Blair's shirt. "Let's get all tangled up in these sheets."

"That's an offer too good to resist." Blair turned back the sheets and finished undressing.

†

Sunlight peeking through the camper window woke Haley the next morning. She was surprised that she had slept through sunrise. Beth would probably arrive midmorning, and she wanted to get more research done. She knew if she went back to the pit, Beth would have a difficult time pulling her away, so Haley turned on the coffee pot and pulled out steaks she would cook for a romantic dinner. Well, as romantic as she could make it in the woods of southern Mississippi.

She poured a coffee and couldn't help but break into a smile when she turned on the computer and pulled up the file she had been reading the night before. She looked at the clock. One hour, then she would need to shower and get ready for Beth's arrival.

"This stuff is just too amazing," she whispered as she continued to scroll down the page, reviewing the images she had downloaded the night before. Haley was engrossed by the information and was startled by the alarm on her cell phone. "An hour can't be up already," she groaned as she reached to turn it off.

She began shedding her clothes as she walked to the small bathroom and turned the shower on. The hot water wouldn't last long, so Haley stepped in and bathed quickly, finishing just as the temperature started to cool. She grabbed a towel, wrapped it around her body, and then surrounded her head with a smaller cloth. She took two steps into the bedroom and caught a glimpse of movement in the corner of her eye. Her heart pounded in her chest. She thought she had locked the door before heading to the shower, but someone was inside the camper. She grabbed the pistol from the bedside table and stepped into the small living area.

Beth looked up at her from the small table and blanched when she saw the gun in Haley's hand.

"Beth," Haley squealed. "You scared the shit out of me. I thought the door was locked, and you wouldn't be here for another hour."

Beth stood and walked toward her, wrapping Haley in her arms. "I couldn't sleep. So, I got an early start. I'm sorry I scared you." She took a step backward and looked at the gun in her lover's hand. "Is everything okay?"

Haley looked down at the gun in her hand and then placed it on the table. "I got a little spooked during the storm last night, and being out here by myself."

"Well, you're not alone anymore, but I can't stay all weekend like we planned."

"What? I thought you didn't have to return until Monday night."

"That was the plan. I've been waiting for weeks for a special lab slot to open up. I was called yesterday and offered the opportunity."

Haley tried to hide the disappointment, but Beth recognized it right away.

"I'm sorry to cut our weekend short, but this was an opportunity too good to pass on."

"I understand. We both have to do what's best for our careers. How long will you be able to stay?"

"Until early afternoon tomorrow."

"Wow. Okay. Did you have anything for breakfast?"

"I went through a drive-thru for a biscuit. Food is the last thing on my mind right now." She pulled Haley close and unwrapped the towel around her waist as she bent down to kiss her. Beth tossed the linen across the back of the chair and broke the kiss.

"Should we take this to the bedroom?"

"Yes, but let me make sure the door is locked this time."

†

Haley snuggled into Beth's arms after their passionate lovemaking. "I'm so glad you were able to come down this weekend, even if it is for a short time. I've missed you."

"I've missed you also. My days seem to drag without you. How are you coming with the dig?"

Haley raised up on an elbow and looked down at her lover. "I had a gut feeling that I was on to something special, and yesterday I believe I hit the jackpot."

Beth smiled up at her. "What did you find?"

"I uncovered two ceremonial knives yesterday. I was doing research last night when the storm moved in, but I think they are a part of some sort of ceremony performed by the Natchez Native American tribe in the seventeen hundreds."

"Wow, that sounds pretty significant," Beth said. "I'm proud of you, honey."

"Thanks. I hope Professor Thomas is as well when she returns next week. If what I've uncovered in the research is correct, the history of the carvings leads all the way up the Mississippi River to the modern-day Illinois area."

"Can you show me what you've found?"

"Absolutely, but I need to rinse off first. I'd invite you, but the shower is incredibly small, and the water supply is limited." She smiled at her lover. "I can show you the find while we wait for the water to re-heat."

†

Casper climbed from his bed and walked over to wash his face at the small sink. He wiped his face and hands on a small towel, and his eyes came to rest on his notepad. Casper stepped over to the small table and picked up the names that he had jotted down the night before.

"So, I wasn't dreaming," he spoke. The chime sounded to alert him to breakfast. His food slot would open soon as a meal tray would be passed through. Until then, he would add some notes to his list while the memories were still fresh. He wrote down the name, *Alice Carmichael, Mississippi.* "Now that was a tasty little prize," he said and chuckled to himself.

The slot dropped open, and his tray was pushed through.

"Mornin', Casper," a friendly voice said as he walked over to retrieve his tray.

"I hope it will be, Roger," Casper said as he took his food tray.

"Will you have the results of your appeal today?"

"There's a possibility," he answered.

"Good luck then, man." The metal slot door slammed shut.

Casper carried the tray of food to his small table and sat. He pushed the notepad to the side and picked up his spoon. The powdered eggs and limp bacon were nothing compared to the hearty meals in the oil fields. Then again, he was no longer that man.

†

Blair loaded the breakfast dishes into the dishwasher as Tally poured them another round of coffee. "What do you want to do today?" she asked Tally.

"I think we should spend the day lounging on the deck unless you want to go down and lay out by the beach."

Blair took the cup of coffee from Tally. "I'm perfectly content with the sun deck. We won't have to deal with the sand getting everywhere, and we'll have the convenience of a bathroom and kitchen just steps away."

"I agree, and we're close enough to watch the surf," Tally replied. "The water's a bit too cool for me, so being on the deck reduces the temptation to get wet."

"I can think of much more enjoyable ways to get you wet," Blair teased.

"There is that, too." Tally grinned. "We're only a few steps from our bedroom."

†

"Those are really beautiful," Beth said as Haley described the intricate carvings on the bone knife handles.

"From what I've been able to discover so far, they belonged to the primary Chief and his brother the War Chief. I haven't uncovered the ritual or ceremony they would have

50

been used together for, but I think this mystery is just beginning."

Beth could see the excitement in Haley's face and hear it in her voice as she spoke about her find. "Do you want to spend the day on your dig?"

"I'll get back on it tomorrow after you leave. I want to spend our time together since we have so little time."

"I'm sorry that the weekend will be cut short, but I need to get this lab session knocked out before I graduate."

"I know, sweetheart, you have to jump on every opportunity you can."

"Will you show me your dig site?"

Haley stood and offered Haley her hand. "Sure, I need to check it to make sure last night's storm didn't damage anything."

She led Beth into the midmorning sun and across the field to her dig site. The ever-present owl sat on the trunk of a dead tree and watched them approach. When she pointed him out, Beth gasped.

"That is one big owl."

"He's been watching over me ever since I started this dig site."

"Doesn't he creep you out just a bit?"

"Not during daylight hours, but the noises he makes at night when he's hunting send shivers down my spine. There are also coyotes in the area that make a bunch of noise."

"Is that what had you spooked last night," Beth asked.

Haley nodded. She left out the feeling of being watched that had also put her nerves on edge. Haley didn't want Beth to worry about her overactive imagination.

"Well, shit," she cried out when they reached the dig. One corner of the tarp had pulled loose, and rainwater had soaked the site. "Help me peel the rest of the tarp back so the sun can dry this out today. I don't cherish wallowing in mud tomorrow."

†

Blair cracked open an eye to check on Tally. Her skin glowed with the tanning oil as she laid on her stomach and napped. The sun brought out the natural tones of her Native American coloring, deepening her skin color. Blair nearly chuckled at the difference between them. Tally tanned so quickly, while her own skin turned pink, and then red before peeling away any chance for color.

Tally must have sensed being watched and opened her eyes to find Blair looking at her. "Is everything okay?"

"I was just admiring how beautifully your body tans compared to my spots of freckles. I feel like I'm baking."

Tally raised her head. "You are turning a little pink. I think it's time to get you inside."

"I'll go inside and shower while you continue to enjoy the sun. I know how much you miss it when we are busy with a case. I'll prepare some sandwiches and let you know when everything is ready."

"Sound great. I'll be right here waiting," Tally said and stretched before rolling onto her back.

Blair stood and looked at the scar on Tally's left forearm that seemed to glow in the bright sunlight. She had been struck by lightning when she was twelve, and the injury was a reminder of the event that triggered the onset of her gift of second sight. Tally had told her how people had treated her because of her differences, and it never failed to make Blair's blood boil. Tally had used her gift to save so many, and give comfort and closure to families that would probably never come to grips with the untimely death of a loved one. Blair had no doubt that people could be so cruel. She and Tally dealt with it every day. She shook the thought from her head and walked inside to shower.

†

Casper heard the slot slide open on his cell.

"You have a visitor," a gruff voice said from outside his door. "Assume the position."

Casper opened his Bible and took out the letter he had written. He was compliant in walking to the door and turning around to position his hands behind his back. He hated this part of his treatment, capitulating power to someone he despised. It always reminded him of the way his stepdad had treated him as a child. The frequent beatings and verbal berating for failing to do something his stepdad desired had left more than physical scars on Casper, some that would not appear until his mid-twenties. He shook the memory of the man he despised. His only regret was not exacting his revenge before being incarcerated. He should have dealt him a dose of his own brand of cruelty, but Casper never got around to doing so. He pulled his cuffed hands out of the slot and heard the snap of the lock that opened his door. Casper turned to face the guard waiting outside his door. *He's just another ugly new face. The turnover in this place is horrendous.*

"Another newbie." He smiled at the guard.

"Just new to the unit. Let's get a move on, Caruso," the guard growled.

Casper felt the hand on his back, propelling him forward, and started walking down the corridor.

When they reached the conference room, and the guard opened the door, he smiled at the attractive attorney. "Good evening, Ms. Herman."

"Mr. Caruso," she nodded as he was cuffed to the table. "You probably know what news I have to deliver."

"Yes. I'm sure my final plea for an appeal was turned down," Casper answered.

"Without hesitation. I requested your execution date be set per your instructions. The judge complied and set a date for December 12."

Casper felt a shiver run through him. The date was barely two months away. He thought he would feel relief to finally know the outcome, but he felt a wave of panic rise inside him. He pushed it back down and looked her in the eyes. "I'm sure you did everything you could to be persuasive and plead my case for an appeal. There's one thing more I need you to do for me."

"What is it?" she asked.

"In my back pocket, I have a letter I would like you to send to Special Agent Blair Cooper at the FBI."

Patricia stood to walk around the table. "Isn't she the agent that finally tracked you down?"

"Yes. Cooper and that freaky psychic she works with," he growled.

She reached down to take the small envelope from his pocket.

"Boo," he hissed at her and then laughed as she jumped back.

"That wasn't funny." She glared at him as she returned to her seat and opened the envelope. "You know I have to get this approved by the prison before I can send it?"

"Yes, but hopefully, I can trust that you will send it. I must meet with Cooper to give her the information on other victims she was never able to tie me to. Since I have no time left or hope of ever leaving this place alive, it's the only humane thing I have left in me. I can give her names and locations where ten more victims are located."

"Why would you do this now?"

"My time is short. If those families are going to get any closure, it has to be now. They can only kill me once, so why take that information with me to my grave?"

"I would say that was compassionate of you, but I don't think you have that in you. I'm sure you have an ulterior motive, but if the prison approves it, I'll send it to the agent."

"That's all I ask."

She stood and straightened her skirt. "This will be the last we see of each other, Mr. Caruso. I hope God has more mercy on you than you had for your victims."

"I don't count on that, Ms. Herman, but thanks for your kind words."

"Goodbye," she said, and took his letter and left the conference room.

Casper listened to the click of her heels on the corridor floor as she made a hasty exit. The guard entered and switched his cuffs for transport back to his cell.

"Did you get the news you were expecting?"

"Yes, I now know the date of my death," Casper answered, and remained silent until he returned to his cell. He rubbed his wrists where the cuffs had been and walked over to the wall to a small prison-made calendar and flipped to December. Casper used his pencil to circle the 12th day of the month.

"What a way to celebrate a Friday night," he said as he dropped the pages of the calendar.

†

Blair had made a stack of sandwiches while Tally was rinsing off in the shower. She poured drinks and picked up the remote to the television just as Tally entered the room. When Blair looked up to the TV, she turned up the volume.

"Son of a bitch."

Tally's eyes flew to the television screen, and she felt faint as she recognized the face on the TV as the same man in her vision. "Who is that?" she asked.

"Hang on a second?" Blair said.

Casper Caruso flashed under the picture of the handsome blond man, and then an attractive red-haired woman was approached by a reporter outside of the Huntsville State Penitentiary.

The reporter's voice broke the silence. "Ms. Herman, can you give us an update on Caruso's final appeal?"

The woman looked into the camera and spoke in a confident voice. "Mr. Caruso, also known as the Ghost of East Texas, has been denied his final appeal for his case. Per his instruction, his execution date has been set for December 12. He has also asked that a letter be delivered to the agent in charge of his case. He wishes to meet with her to discuss multiple other victims before his execution." Patricia lifted the envelope into view.

"Is this just a ploy to extend his execution?" the reporter asked.

"Since he asked for his date to be set, I don't believe that is his motivation. I think a glimmer of humanity still exists within him, and he wants to provide closure for several grieving families."

"So, he's basically admitting to several additional murders?"

"Yes, but as he stated, 'they can only kill me once, so I've nothing to lose.'"

"Will we be hearing more about these alleged victims?"

"That depends on the validity of his claims and the FBI."

"Thank you for your update, Ms. Herman," the reporter said, and the camera switched to the reporter's face. "This news was far from expected, so stay tuned for future updates on the Ghost of East Texas victims."

"Well, I'll be damned." Blair took a seat at the table. "I sure didn't expect that from him."

Tally joined her at the table. "Blair."

Blair looked at Tally. "Yes, love?"

"That was the man in my vision."

"At least that part of the riddle is solved. I wonder what Casper is really up to with this stunt?"

Tally's next words startled her. "He wants his last fifteen minutes of fame before he leaves this world."

"You think so?"

"I know he doesn't possess an ounce of remorse for any of his victims. So why now for any other reason than to put him back in the spotlight?"

"That does make sense. Does it help to shed any other light on the rest of your visions?"

"Not a clue on those, but putting a name to his face is a start. You will go to Texas to talk to him, right?"

"I'm almost positive the boss will have me booked when we return next week. It would look bad if the agency turned down an opportunity to provide closure for some families."

"I want to go with you. I think I need to be there to help."

"I was hoping you'd say that. Caruso is a clever man, and he won't make this an easy reveal, if nothing else, to keep himself in the news."

"I think you need to turn your phone back on, Blair."

Blair walked over to the counter where the phone sat idle and powered it back on. Several messages flashed on her screen, the first from her father, read, *If you haven't seen the news coming out of Texas, google Casper Caruso.*

The second was from the agency's head, requesting she check her encrypted mail and give him a call. Blair opened the email and read it to Tally.

"We have both been invited to meet with him. I'm sorry, but you know this will probably cut our vacation short."

"That's fine. If we can help some grieving families, it's worth the time. I'll start packing while you make the call."

"Wait until I'm done. I'm going to ask for one more night. We can head home tomorrow and drive into the office, then fly out Monday."

Tally nodded and picked up a sandwich as Blair dialed her phone and walked out to the deck.

†

"I'm impressed by the work you've done here, babe," Beth told Haley as they walked back to the camper.

"I'm on the verge of our first big find here," Haley answered. "It's not like discovering King Tut, but it's hopefully going to reveal a bit more of our history and culture in America."

"I think it's going to be very important. I can see that it's really stoked your fire for future digs. You seem more excited about your studies than ever."

"I needed this to confirm archeology was what I was born to do. Now I know," Haley said as she slipped her hand into Beth's. "Speaking of stoking fires, I have steaks to cook for dinner, and then we can build a campfire for tonight."

"That sounds great. I bet it's even more beautiful here at night. You can actually see the stars in the sky."

"Yes, you can, and they are beautiful."

CHAPTER FOUR

Blair and Tally showered before carrying their bags to the car. Blair placed them in the trunk and turned to Tally.

"I'm sad we had to cut this trip short, but thank you for being here with me."

"It was a great time. I loved being here with you. Maybe we can return at a later time and enjoy a full vacation."

Blair sighed. "Only time will tell. There's no telling what kind of wild goose hunt Caruso is going to send us on."

"We'll deal with whatever he throws us. If it gives more families a slight sense of closure, it's worth the time."

Blair smiled. "I know you're right, but that man gives me the creeps. I hate that you will be forced to meet with him, but his letter specifically asked for you."

"That probably means he plans some fun and games," Tally said as she walked to the car door and opened it. "At least I'll be with you."

"That's a good point. Have you ever been to Texas?" Blair asked.

"Nope, this will be another first for me." Tally grinned and climbed into the car.

†

Haley was sad to see Beth leave, but she was also eager to spend whatever daylight she had left working on the dig. After a long kiss goodbye, Haley returned to the camper for her pistol and tools. She clipped the holster to her belt and started across the field. The sun seemed to be in hyperdrive as it headed to the horizon. "Not much time left today," Haley spoke aloud as she looked down into the pit. "At least the sun and heat dried it out a bit."

†

Haley was about to step into the pit when movement caught the corner of her vision. She snapped her head around in time to see a young woman staring at her. The hairs on Haley's arms stood on end. The young woman looked like she had been beaten, her clothes were torn and ragged. Haley knew there were no homes within twenty miles of the dig site. The appearance of this young woman seemed so odd. Haley took a step toward her, and the woman turned away but looked back at her. Haley cautiously looked around for anyone else in the area, but there was no one else in sight.

61

She had an eerie feeling something was not right with this woman, but she couldn't help but follow her deeper into the woods. Haley reached down and unsnapped the holster to her pistol as she took tentative steps toward the woman.

†

"Home sweet home," Blair said as they pulled into the garage. Her phone pinged, and she had a message that included two electronic tickets for her and Tally. "We can drive into the office early in the morning. We have until two to get briefed and get to the airport." She frowned when she saw the look on Tally's face. "I know you hate flying."

Tally shrugged. "Will I ever get used to flying?"

"Hopefully, one day. I'd love to take you to some faraway islands somewhere without cell phone reception." Blair chuckled.

"That's a good incentive," Tally smiled at her. "Maybe I can just take a quick nap while we're in the air."

"That sounds like a good plan. I don't think we'll be getting much sleep for the next few days."

"Why don't I call for some Chinese delivery while you start packing," Tally suggested. "We can eat and relax this evening and head out early in the morning."

"That's a great idea. I'll go ahead and take our bags to the car once they are packed."

†

Haley felt a cold sweat break out on her face as the woman stopped and pointed. Haley's eyes turned in the direction the woman was pointing and gasped when she saw a skeleton, partially leaning against a massive tree. She turned to look back at the woman, but she was gone. Haley turned in a complete circle, but the woman was nowhere to be seen. She stepped forward cautiously, removing the pistol from her holster as she approached. Haley saw a woman's purse several yards away from the skeleton, and when her eyes scanned the tree, Haley stopped in her tracks. She recognized the material of the clothing held in place by a disintegrating piece of rope as the same color blouse the woman had been wearing. Had she just seen the woman's ghost?

†

Decomposition had long claimed the flesh from the body, but Haley retched as she realized she had been led to a murder scene. She walked quickly away and dropped to her knees out of sight of the tree. Her fingers were shaking violently as Haley reached for her cell phone, praying there would be service. Her hand steadied enough to see that she had three bars.

"Thank God," she whispered and dialed 911.

†

"I think I have finally acquired the talent of using chopsticks," Tally bragged as she lifted a chunk of honey chicken to her mouth. She took a quick bite before her luck or skill ran out.

63

"We've had a good bit of practice in the last few months, but I'm very proud of you," Blair told her.

"I think we should shower and go to bed once we finish here," Tally suggested.

Blair glanced at the clock. She smiled when she saw it was at eight o'clock. "That sounds great to me."

†

Within thirty minutes, the area where Haley was located filled with flashing red and blue lights. A detective had placed her in the passenger seat of his SUV and was asking her the same set of questions he had earlier.

"Why are we repeating these questions?" she asked.

"I want to make sure you haven't left anything out. You know your story about being led here by a ghost is a hard pill for a policeman to swallow," he told her with a smile.

"Do you think, th-th-that I could have anything to do with this?" Haley stuttered.

"Absolutely not. I'm sorry if you thought that, but I think in terms of hard evidence, and a woman that disappears into thin air is difficult to believe."

"I swear that is exactly what happened." Haley felt flushed. When she looked away from him, she saw a uniformed officer leading someone toward the car. She gasped when she saw it was Dr. Thomas. "Can I go?"

"Yes, don't go far. We may have a few other questions."

†

Haley bolted from the car, and Dr. Thomas reached for her. "I am so glad to see you."

"I decided to head back early. When I saw all these flashing lights, and could not find you, I thought I'd better investigate. Are you alright?"

"Yes, ma'am. It has been a strange day," Haley said.

"Do you want to tell me about it?"

Haley nodded and began the story of coming out to the site after Beth left to do some more digging when she saw the young woman. Dr. Thomas shook her head when Haley told her about the woman disappearing.

"You saw a ghost?" Dr. Thomas asked.

"I don't know how else to describe her. She led me here and simply disappeared."

"Can we get you back to your camper? I think we both need something strong to drink."

"I don't know if I can go yet," Haley stated.

"Let me handle this."

Haley watched her approach a detective Haley had been talking to. She saw Dr. Thomas point in the direction of their campsite, and then nod to the man.

When Dr. Thomas returned, she smiled softly to Haley. "Let's go back to camp. They know how to reach us if needed."

The moon had risen to light their path, but Haley insisted on using her flashlight. As they crossed through the field to the dig site, the owl screeched and took flight. Haley could feel a cold streak of fear wash over her.

"We definitely need a shot of whiskey after that. That owl scared the bejeesus out of me." Dr. Thomas led Haley over to her motor home and unlocked the door. "Take a seat."

Haley took a seat at the small dining table that also functioned as a desk for Dr. Thomas. She looked up when the older woman approached and handed her a glass half-filled with a dark liquid.

"I hope you like Jack Daniels."

Haley took a deep sip and felt the liquid burn as it rushed down her throat. "Jack isn't my favorite, but he sure hits the spot tonight."

"Go slow, but I've got plenty more," Dr. Thomas said. "I've found a good drink of Jack will settle nerves any time." She took a sip. "I can't imagine the scare you've had today. Most of the remains we uncover are hundreds or thousands of years old."

Haley nodded. "That's definitely what I signed up for when I chose this field. The detective told me the young woman had been missing for fifteen years. Incredibly, her driver's license was still in her purse after all these years."

"At least the family may gain some closure now that she's been located. It's still hard, but at least they can give her a proper burial."

Haley looked up and saw the tears in Dr. Thomas' eyes. She wondered if she had gone through something similar.

Dr. Thomas saw her questioning look. "Yes, I know the feeling from experience. My son Jacob was killed in Desert Storm, but it was months before his remains were recovered. I wasn't at rest until his coffin was lowered into the ground at Arlington. It's still a heartbreak, but at least you know your loved one is home."

"I'm so sorry, Dr. Thomas. I didn't have a clue." Haley smiled at her.

"It was years ago before you even got to the university. Jacob died doing what he wanted to do. Ever since he was a young boy, he dreamed of being a marine and serving his country."

They fell silent for several minutes as they sipped the strong liquor. Dr. Thomas looked up. "I don't have much for groceries, but I do have some cheese and crackers. Would you join me for a snack?"

"Only if you let me add some lunchmeat to it from my stash." Haley grinned. "I'll be right back."

Haley returned to her camper and grabbed a package of ham and two soft drinks. The whiskey had calmed her nerves, but the last thing she needed right now was a hangover to top this horrible night.

†

"I'm so glad you don't mind driving in this rat race," Tally said as Blair wove through early morning traffic.

"Years of practice." She grinned and turned into the complex.

After they parked and entered the building, they were directed straight into the director's office.

"I'm sorry to ask you ladies to cut your vacation short, but this is a very time-sensitive investigation. Caruso's execution date has been set for December 12, so we have less than two months to glean all the information from him we can. He's claiming he can lead you to ten more victims."

Blair and Tally took a seat across from him.

"Also, there has been a change in plans this morning. A new case has come in that we think might include one of Caruso's victims."

"Really? Where?" Blair asked.

"In southern Mississippi," he answered. "An archeology student has a rather odd story, but she located the body of Alice Carmichael from Hattiesburg that has been missing for fifteen years. Carmichael fits Caruso's profile entirely."

Tally stiffened when the director mentioned an archeology student. She wondered if that was the young woman she had seen in her vision.

Blair sensed her tension and looked at Tally. "Are you okay?"

"One of the people in my vision was a young woman I presumed to be an archeologist working at a dig site," Tally explained.

"That's precisely why we have booked you a flight into Jackson. An agent will pick you up and take you to the scene. The young lady says she was led to the discovery by the woman's ghost. If anyone can understand that and help her, I think it would be you, Ms. Rainwater."

"I understand," Tally replied. "It may also be helpful to visit the site if she was one of his victims."

The director looked at Blair. "You will fly into Texas and begin discussions with Caruso. As soon as Ms. Rainwater is done in Mississippi, she will be transported to Huntsville to assist." He took a deep breath. "This could be very important for ten families if you can bring their loved ones home. I know you'll give it your best effort. Caruso asked for the two of you, so be prepared for some of his challenges. He's intelligent, but can't out-think both of you.

You leave at two. Ms. Rainwater, my secretary, Eliza, has your new itinerary. Good luck and keep me posted, please."

"Yes, sir," Blair responded, and they turned to leave.

"Be sure to try the beef brisket in Texas. It's supposed to be the best in the world."

"Will do," Blair responded as they left his office.

After stopping to get Tally's itinerary, they walked to Blair's office. "Do you feel okay about going to Mississippi by yourself?"

Tally smiled. "I'm a big girl, and before I met you, I traveled alone."

"I know you did, but I love you and don't want you to do anything you're not comfortable with."

"I'm fine and won't be more than a day or so behind you. Maybe I can gather some information that might rattle his cage a bit if he starts getting cheeky," Tally offered.

"Ms. Rainwater, I do believe you might have a devilish streak in you," Blair said.

"It would be a pleasure to beat him at his own game." Tally grinned.

"Okay, so let's grab what we need here, eat a nice lunch, and head to the airport." Blair pulled out a thick file on Caruso and placed it in her briefcase and a fresh pad and pens. "Do you need anything?"

"Nope, I've got my notebook and laptop already packed," Tally answered.

"Okay, so the next big decision is lunch."

"Let's hit the steak place out by the airport," Tally suggested.

"Perfect," Blair answered, and they left the building.

†

Haley woke the next morning and was surprised to find Dr. Thomas sipping coffee in front of her motor home. "I was going to make some breakfast if you'd care to join me."

"Anything other than a pop tart would be lovely," she answered.

Haley chuckled. "No pop tarts here. How about toast and some scrambled eggs. Sorry, but my bacon is frozen."

"That would be wonderful, thanks."

"Come on in when you get ready. I've got a pot of coffee brewing."

"Creamer?" Dr. Thomas asked.

"French vanilla," Haley replied.

"Perfect. I'm on my way."

Haley watched her approach and they stepped inside.

"How are you feeling this morning?" Dr. Thomas asked.

"Like I woke up from a bad dream," Haley admitted.

"Hopefully, there won't be much more needed from you. I noticed there is a newly started pit. Is that yours?"

"Holy shit," Haley said. "I'm sorry."

"No worries, I've said shit thousands of times." Dr. Thomas chuckled.

"With everything that happened, I forgot to tell you about what I've found. Come in and have a seat while I get coffee, and I'll show you." She pointed Dr. Thomas to her small dining room table.

Haley poured them a fresh cup and carried it to the table. Then she walked into her room and brought a bundle wrapped in a soft towel to the table. "I had a feeling about that area. Something was drawing me to the spot and, so far, this is what I've found." She unwrapped the bundle, and Dr. Thomas gasped.

"These are gorgeous," she said, carefully turning the blades over on the towel.

"I've started some research and found some interesting information." Haley pushed a key to bring her laptop from sleep mode and pulled up a collection of files. "You can browse these while I cook."

Dr. Thomas looked up at her. "Fantastic."

†

Tally walked to the baggage claim and saw a young man in a suit pacing the area, looking for someone. "Are you Agent Carson," she asked.

"Oh, yes, ma'am. Are you Ms. Rainwater?"

"Tally," she said and offered him her hand.

"Jamie." He smiled and took her hand. "I am to be your escort for the next few days," he explained. "I, uh, was expecting someone older."

"If it makes you feel better, I was, too." Tally grinned at him.

Jamie returned her grin. "I've only been out of the academy a few months."

Tally saw her bags on the conveyor belt. She moved around him to grab them.

"Here, let me get those for you," he said. "Just point them out to me."

Tally pointed out her two bags, and he collected them. She followed him out into the bright sunshine and put on her sunglasses.

Jamie had used his FBI parking pass to park on the curb, so they walked directly to the black SUV. He placed her bags in the back and opened the door for her. When he climbed in behind the wheel, he started the engine.

"I've read up on your work. You seem amazing. I think it's terrific the FBI is beginning to realize the importance of using psychic assistance on cases. Your recovery rate and rescues have been astonishing."

"Thanks," Tally said. "Agent Cooper and I make a good team."

He nodded. "Agent Cooper is becoming a legend, just like her father."

"Don't tell her that when you meet her. She's very humble and feels like she's just doing her job."

"I get to meet her?" Jamie asked.

"If you are assigned to take me to Huntsville, Texas, you will. We are interviewing Casper Caruso to see if he can lead us to another ten victims before he's executed."

"I saw that on the news and on the Bureau webpage. I'd love to stay and watch y'all work, but my orders are to deliver you and head home."

"We'll see about that. How long until we reach the crime scene?"

"About two and a half hours," he answered after checking his GPS.

"So, tell me about yourself, Agent Carson," Tally grinned.

†

Blair touched down in Texas and was met by a female agent at the gate. She had to check her weapon, so that was a prearranged meeting spot. Blair walked up to find the attractive young woman waiting for her arrival.

"Agent Cooper. It's so great to meet you. I'm Linda Enzo, and I'm your escort today. After you collect your weapon, we'll get your luggage." The woman looked around. "Is Ms. Rainwater not with you?"

Blair chuckled. "She'll be here in a couple days. She got rerouted to Mississippi."

"I see." The young agent waited for Blair to receive her sidearm, and they proceeded to baggage claim.

"Is it as hot as it looks?" Blair asked as they walked toward the baggage claim exit. She could see waves of heat shimmering off the pavement.

"It's a scorcher out there, but I've got great air conditioning in the vehicle. Would you like something cold to drink? I've got a cooler full of water in the back."

Blair nodded. "That would be perfect."

They loaded her bag in the rear of the vehicle, and Linda removed two bottles of water from the cooler. She handed a bottle to Blair.

"All set?"

"I believe so. How long before we get to Huntsville?"

Linda looked at Blair. "I've been ordered to check you into your hotel and then take you out to the institution in the morning. The ride to Huntsville will be about an hour, depending on traffic."

"That sounds good. It's probably too late to visit today."

"I've arranged a visitation room for you tomorrow at nine," Linda replied. "The hotel is only ten minutes away from Huntsville prison. They have a decent restaurant, and there are several chain eateries close. Do you want me to arrange a vehicle for you?"

"That should be fine. Once Tally arrives, we may want a vehicle, but as long as you're willing to chauffer me, I'm good."

Linda returned her smile. "I'll take you anywhere you wish to go."

"So, tell me about yourself," Blair said, hoping to pass the time during the drive.

†

"You've uncovered an amazing find," Dr. Thomas said as Haley placed a plate filled with steaming eggs and buttered toast in front of her.

"I've got some orange juice if you'd like?"

"No, this is good," Dr. Thomas answered. Her eyes never left the screen until Haley sat down. "So, what do you think you've uncovered?"

Haley beamed at her. "I think it's some form of a burial site, and I'm hoping we can recover a body. What is curious to me is, if it were one of the Chief's, why would they be buried here instead of at Emerald Mound?"

"That is an excellent question. One would assume that with the importance of the weapons you found. That does seem curious. Are you up to work this morning, and may I assist?"

Haley was so excited she could barely sit still. "I would be honored to work with you."

"Let's finish eating and get out there before the sun starts to bake us." She shook her head. "It just hit me that I have a large canopy that we can put over the site to give us shade and protect it from the elements."

"That would be great. I've got a couple of camp chairs we can carry down, too." Haley smiled.

✝

Jamie took a look at Tally. "We will be arriving shortly. It's pretty remote, so if you want a snack or something to drink, we need to stop soon."

"I could use a bathroom break and a snack," Tally replied.

"That's no problem." Jamie turned on his blinker and exited to a truck stop. "This should work for anything you need." He dropped her at the front of the store. "I'm going to top off the fuel, and I'll meet you inside."

"Thanks, Jamie," Tally said and left the vehicle. She walked inside and located the restroom right away. Tally had selected a cold drink and was browsing the snack section when Jamie found her.

"I'll use the restroom, and then I'll be ready whenever you are." He smiled sweetly to her.

"I'll meet you in the front," Tally said. She picked out a snack cake and walked to the counter to make her purchases. *My body must think I'm going to need all this sugar. Blair would be laughing by now.* The thought of Blair made her smile. She nibbled on the snack while she waited for Jamie to join her.

"All set?" he asked.

"Just waiting on you," Tally grinned.

"Let's do this."

†

Haley stood and stretched her back muscles. She and Dr. Thomas had been crouched in the pit for several hours. Their efforts had been rewarded when the first glimmer of bone shone through the dark soil.

"Shit, I forgot my camera," she cried out. "I'll be right back."

Dr. Thomas smiled. "Let's take some pictures and take a break to ride into town for something to eat. My eggs are long gone, and I need to pick up a few supplies."

Haley's smile faded, and Dr. Thomas noticed.

"Never mind, you take photos and continue, and I'll go to town. I'll bring lunch and supplies back while you continue to work. I forgot how exciting it was to have your first find. Enjoy, and continue to take photos. I promise I won't be gone long." She climbed out of the pit and pulled her gloves from her hands.

They walked together to the campsite. Dr. Thomas turned to Haley. "Are you good with some fried chicken and the fixings?"

"Perfect," Haley replied. "May I offer to pay?"

"Not necessary, but thank you. We need to celebrate your find." Dr. Thomas grinned.

Haley smiled back at her. "Thank you." Haley walked into her camper to retrieve her camera.

Dr. Thomas was pulling away and tossed her hand out the window to wave. Haley waved and rushed back to the pit.

She pulled on her gloves and picked up a variety of tools before entering the dig. The heat waves shimmered from the ground, and Haley noted the cool breeze that had bathed them in comfort had disappeared. She felt a bead of sweat roll down her forehead, down the bridge of her nose. She exhaled sharply and sent the droplet sailing. The T-shirt was beginning to cling to her back, so Haley pulled it over her head and tossed it onto a camp chair. The sports bra was the only thing remaining, and Haley could feel the instant respite from the heat. Surely Dr. Thomas would be gone for an hour or more. Then they would break to eat during the heat of the day. Haley snapped several photos with her camera from a variety of angles then picked up a brush to begin moving the dirt from around the bone.

Her heart raced when she realized she was slowly uncovering a hand. The hand looked too small to be an adult male, but it appeared to be intact, as digit after digit were revealed, stopping for photographs every few minutes. Haley continued working until she heard the vehicle's approach and looked up to find Dr. Thomas had returned. Haley climbed from the pit and removed her gloves before slipping the shirt back over her body. Then she walked over to help carry bags inside. She looked at the large container of fried chicken, red beans and rice, and coleslaw and grinned.

"Yeah, I must have been hungry. Oh well, what we don't eat we can have for dinner," Dr. Thomas said as she saw Haley's grin. "Let's get this stuff inside. The smell has been driving me crazy for twenty minutes."

Haley chuckled and picked up the last of the bags. She had to admit, the aroma coming from the chicken had her mouth watering, too.

†

It was nearly six when Blair was checked into her room. Linda had left her card with her cell number on the back.

"Call me if you need anything. Otherwise, I will meet you at eight in the lobby."

"Thanks, Linda. I'll see you in the morning."

The valet had taken her bags and placed them in her room. Blair tipped him and stepped inside a spacious suite with a king-sized bed, an ample spot for a workstation, and a huge garden tub with jets. She was pleased to see a stand-alone shower in the corner. *That tub will get some use when Tally arrives,* she thought. Blair returned to the bedroom and began unpacking her clothes. Luckily, the slacks and blouses had survived the flight with the same crispness they had when she had packed them. She hung them in the walk-in closet and stored her bags. Her stomach growled loudly, announcing it was time to consider a meal. Blair picked up the room service list and perused the limited selection. She understood the full menu would be available in the restaurant to entice guests to spend more money. *I'm on the government's dime, so it's the restaurant for me.* Blair picked up her key card and headed for the elevator.

†

Haley and Dr. Thomas had returned to the site after stuffing themselves with fried chicken. They had worked together to uncover bones up to an elbow when they saw a black SUV pull into the campsite.

"I wonder who that could be?" Dr. Thomas asked as two sharply dressed passengers, young man and woman, emerged from the vehicle. "They are definitely not students. I'll be right back."

Haley watched her approach the visitors and saw Dr. Thomas point toward the dig site after talking with them for several minutes. The young woman left the group and began walking toward her. She was petite in size and scanned the area with her eyes as she approached. Haley stepped out of the pit.

"Haley?" the woman asked.

"Yes, I'm Haley. What can I do for you?"

The young woman smiled as she stepped under the canopy. "My name is Tally Rainwater, and I am a consultant with the FBI. I would like to speak with you about the events from yesterday, if possible."

"Are you an FBI Agent?" Haley asked.

Tally nodded toward Jamie. "I'm not, but he is. I work with the FBI as a consultant on cases."

Haley brushed off the sand from a camp chair and motioned to Tally.

Tally took her seat, and, now under the shade, removed her sunglasses. She saw the slight recoil when the young woman looked in her eyes. She couldn't stifle a chuckle.

Haley blushed furiously for her rude reaction.

"It's okay. I get that reaction all the time. I know it's not often you see someone with two different-colored eyes.

"They are unique," Haley replied with a slight smile.

Tally's eyes drifted into the pit. She took a deep breath and looked at Haley. "What I'm about to tell you may seem very odd, but please hear me out before reacting. Okay?"

79

Haley nodded.

"I'm a psychic, and I normally work with my partner, Agent Blair Cooper, but she has been assigned a case in Texas that we feel may be connected to the young woman you discovered."

"A psychic? Really?" Haley asked.

"Weirdly enough, I've seen you before in my visions. I watched as you discovered the ceremonial knives from this burial site." Haley felt the color drain from her face.

"How could you know that? Only my girlfriend and now Dr. Thomas know about them." Haley was shocked.

Tally leaned toward Haley. "When I was twelve, I was struck by lightning. The trauma triggered the psychic ability I had not been able to explain before. Sometimes, like now, I have visions, snippets really, of actual events, and I have to discover how to place the puzzle pieces together to gain the whole story. It's not unlike what you are doing here," she suggested. "What you discover will eventually lead to a piece of history no one else knows."

"That does make sense, but yesterday was so odd." Haley wiped the sweat from her brow.

"Can you tell me about it?" Tally asked.

"My girlfriend, Beth, had just left to go back to campus. We are students at Mississippi State. I decided to do some more work on the dig after she left." Haley's mouth suddenly felt dry, so she reached for a water bottle and took a sip. "When I arrived here, I felt an odd sense of being watched. It wasn't the first time, but this time I caught movement on the edge of my vision. When I scoured the edge of the woods, I saw a young woman, maybe in her late teens. She looked pale, her clothing was tattered, and she looked bruised like she had been mistreated. I started to walk toward her, and she turned into the forest."

"That was very brave," Tally said.

"For some reason, I felt compelled to follow her. I could never catch up to her no matter how quickly I walked, and then suddenly, she stopped and pointed toward a tree. I glanced at the tree and saw the skeleton leaning partially against it, but when I looked back, she was gone. Disappeared like she had never been there. I wasn't a believer in ghosts before, but I'll swear to my final breath that young woman led me to her remains."

Tally smiled. "I am a believer in ghosts, and what you described is exactly as it appears. The young woman, Alice, wanted you to find her so she could go home. She's been missing for fifteen years."

"I thought I was going crazy, but I believed it to be true," Haley said.

Tally smiled. "Can you take me where she was found?"

Haley nodded. "Yes. Let me tell my professor where I'm going."

"She already knows. I asked about her involvement when we first arrived, and she told me she came in after the fact."

"Let's go then." Haley stood up so abruptly the chair fell backward. "Sorry, I'm a bit nervous."

"It's okay. What you did for Alice is a beautiful thing. You have brought a child home to a mourning family. It's my job now to discover how and why she was taken before her time." Tally lowered her sunglasses and followed Haley.

†

Tally could once more feel the aura of death. She sensed it at the dig site, but what she felt entering the woods felt evil. She felt cold even though it was well in the ninety-degree range. Haley was silent as they walked, and when she stopped and pointed, Tally looked at her.

"I don't think I can go any closer," Haley said.

The area had been cordoned off with crime-scene tape, and a solitary deputy remained on site. Small yellow flags were stuck in the ground, and Tally knew there had been forensic evidence collected from the spots.

"It's okay. Can you wait for me here?"

"Yes, ma'am," Haley nodded, and quickly turned away from the scene.

"I won't be any longer than necessary." Tally placed a hand on her shoulder. "You sure you're okay?"

"Yes," Haley answered with a nod.

Tally approached the deputy who had stepped out of his cruiser and showed him her credentials. He nodded and returned to the comfort of his vehicle.

Tally's eyes scanned the area, and she felt her mind open to the energy remaining. She was surprised when Lisa appeared.

"There you are. I thought you had abandoned me," Tally spoke in her mind.

"No, I've been busy investigating what you are about to walk into in Texas. That is one sick man," she heard Lisa say.

"Blair is even apprehensive about talking with him, but she'll sacrifice her time to bring closure to more families. I get the sense Alice was one of his victims."

"Yes, she was. Step forward and touch the tree." Lisa paused. "It's safe."

Tally walked toward the tree. She could see the indentations from the rope that bound Alice which had cut into the bark. Her fingers felt the energy emanating from the spot as Tally reached forward to place her hand on the tree. As soon as she made contact with the warm surface, her vision came alive like a movie camera. Tally felt the bark's roughness as the images showed Caruso capturing the young woman in a parking lot. Tally could feel Alice's terror as she awoke, bound and gagged in his vehicle. The physical and sexual abuse Alice suffered was unbearable, and Tally cringed from the repeated blows from the monster. She watched as he covered her mouth with a cloth, and her body went limp. Caruso dressed her in her torn clothing and used a thick, rough rope to bind her to the large tree.

When she awoke from the drug, Alice's eyes grew wide with horror as she watched Caruso approach her with a straight razor. Tally could smell the stench of alcohol on his breath as he bent down next to Alice. "You were one fine piece of ass," he growled, and then in a blur of motion, he raked the razor across Alice's throat. Tally could hear his wicked laughter. When the blood started flowing, Tally jerked her hand away from the tree.

Tears flowed freely down her face for the young woman so brutally treated. It took several moments for Tally to regain her composure. When she turned around, she found that Haley had been watching her. On quivering legs, Tally walked over to her. "Take me back to your dig site, please."

†

Haley could see the drawn look and the lack of color on Tally's face. She quickly led her back to the canopy and guided Tally to a seat. She handed her the bottle of water they had left behind.

"Thank you," Tally said and took a long drink. "I was wondering if you could do one more thing for me?"

"Sure, what do you need?"

"Bring me the knives you discovered. There's something here that needs to be explained."

Haley rushed back to her camper. Dr. Thomas and the young FBI agent were seated under her awning, and they looked at her when she rushed out carrying a small bundle.

"We'll be right back," Haley hollered to them and raced back to Tally. She prayed the young psychic could provide more answers to help unravel the mystery of her discovery. Haley sat across from Tally and carefully unwrapped the bundle. She handed Tally both of the blades.

†

Tally could feel the warmth of love emanating from the knives as they touched her skin. Her mind again opened, and she saw the two young girls from her vision. They were beautiful and so obviously in love it made Tally's heart ache for them. The scenes that played out before her eyes were confusing. Thankfully, Lisa showed up to guide her.

"There was a great battle, and the war chief was killed. To enable him to travel into the afterlife, a sacrifice needed to be made to accompany him," Lisa explained. "I'm sorry I cannot tell you what their names were, but the two young women were daughters of the two central chiefs of the tribe, and they were in love. Knowing that their love would not be accepted, they volunteered for the sacrifice. The surviving chief denied their request, so the young lovers took their own lives so they would be together for eternity."

Tally felt the flood of tears as they washed down her face. She removed her glasses and Tally used the towel Haley handed her to wipe her face. She took another long drink of water.

"Are you okay?" Haley asked.

Tally nodded. "I'm fine, and I have something to share with you."

Haley leaned in to hear Tally's soft voice.

"You will find two young native American women in this grave. If I guessed, I'd say they were in their mid-teens. They were the daughters of the two chiefs that ruled over this tribe, but I'm sorry I do not know their names." Tally paused to look up at Haley. Her senses and the discussion of a girlfriend had led Tally to believe Haley was a lesbian and would understand the next part of their conversation.

"The two young women were lovers. When a war chief or primary chief dies or is killed in battle, it is customary for a human to be sacrificed to guide his spirit into the afterlife. The young women knew their love would never be accepted so they volunteered to be the sacrifice, but they were denied by the chief who refused to let his daughter go. Desperate to remain together, the young lovers took the sacrificial knives and slit their wrists. They were buried here together, wrapped in one another's arms, just as they had died." Tally opened her eyes and saw Haley crying. "Don't mourn for them; they died happily and will be forever together."

Haley wiped her eyes with the back of her hand. "You can tell all of that by holding those knives?"

"They act as a trigger. I also have a spirit guide that helps me make sense of the visions I experience. Her name is Lisa, and she knew part of their story."

"That makes sense of the information I've discovered on the internet searching for data on the Natchez tribe. Thank you for filling in some of the blanks."

"Thank you for helping Alice return home, and one day I hope you tell the story of these two young lovers." Tally smiled at her.

Haley stood with Tally. "Did you find out what you needed to know about Alice?"

"Yes, I did. Thank you for telling me your part of this story. You won't have to worry about testifying. The man who killed her is already scheduled for execution in Texas, so there won't be a trial."

"I'm glad he's got what's coming to him for what he did to Alice." Haley forced a smile. "Thank you for aiding me as well. I feel much closer to these women now."

"Good luck unraveling that story." Tally handed Haley a business card. "Keep me posted on your progress if you will."

"Thanks. Will you keep in touch and let me know if you have any other visions?"

"Sure, drop me an email, so I'll have your address."

They walked back toward the campers. "Good luck with your dig. You've got a beautiful spot to work."

"Thanks, good luck in Texas. I hope you get all the questions answered for those families."

"We will do our best."

Jamie stood when they returned. "All set?"

"Yes. Thanks again, Haley. Goodbye for now."

Tally and Jamie loaded into the SUV as darkness started to fall. She waved at Haley, then pulled out her notepad.

"Where to now?" Jamie asked.

"I guess we need to head toward Texas. We can find a hotel and a decent meal along the way."

Jamie grinned. "I know of some great seafood places in Baton Rouge. It's a few hours from here, but on our way."

"Sounds perfect," Tally replied and pulled out her notebook and started jotting down notes.

CHAPTER FIVE

After a meal of char-grilled oysters and fried shrimp, Tally groaned when she lifted her bag onto the curb. "I think I'll sleep like a rock after that meal," she told Jamie.

Jamie went to pull out her other bag. "You can leave that one. I've got everything I need for tonight, right here." She patted her suitcase.

"Here, let me get that for you," Jamie said as he grabbed his small bag and took the handle from Tally.

"You're going to spoil me, Jamie." Tally smiled at him.

"My mama raised me right." They approached the front desk. "Two rooms, please, for one night, at the government rate."

"I'll need to see some credentials," the desk clerk told him.

"No problem." Jamie pulled out his FBI identification.

"I don't have adjoining rooms. Are rooms across from one another good?" the clerk asked.

"That will be fine," Jamie said and handed him a credit card.

The clerk ran his card and handed him two room keys. "There you are. Do you folks need a wake-up call?"

"Thanks, I think we're good," Jamie replied. He handed Tally a card as they started down the hallway. "We've got less than five hours to Huntsville. Do you want to meet at seven in the morning?"

Tally nodded. "That will be great and should allow us to be in Huntsville around lunch."

They stopped in front of their rooms. "Hey, Jamie."

"Ma'am?"

"Who is your supervisor?"

"Director Lewis. Have I done something wrong?" He looked confused.

"Heaven's no. I was going to drop the name to Agent Cooper to see if she could get you approved to spend a few days in Texas. Your victim was a resident of Mississippi. It only seems appropriate that you represent your agency, especially if there may be another resident involved."

Jamie smiled broadly. "I'd love that. I'd have to buy a few new shirts, but it would be well worth spending a few days with the two of you."

"I'll see what I can do." Tally smiled and entered her room. "See you in the morning."

"Goodnight, Tally."

†

Tally was met with a rush of cold air as soon as she stepped inside. "Holy cow," she said when she looked at the thermostat and saw it set to sixty degrees. "You could hang meat in here." She made a quick adjustment and placed her bag on the stand near the large bed. Tally decided to give Blair a call, take a hot shower, and climb into bed. She pulled out her hygiene kit and picked up her cell. Tally sat in a recliner and called Blair.

She placed the phone on the arm of the chair with the speaker on, as she removed her shoes.

"Hey, baby," Blair answered. "Where and how are you?"

"I'm in Baton Rouge. We just checked into the hotel. I'm exhausted, but well. How are you?"

"Tired from a bumpy flight, but I had a good meal, and I'm reviewing my files on Caruso. There is a conference room reserved for me at nine in the morning." She paused for several seconds. "How was your stop in Mississippi?"

"Very informative on several levels. I received some information that might knock Caruso off his pedestal if we need to remind him that he's scheduled for execution soon."

"That sounds good. I can't wait to hear what you found. Is there more?"

Tally chuckled. "You know me too well. Yes, there's more. The young woman that found the knives and the two young Native American women from my vision also played a role in my trip. It's all good, and to be honest, I'm too tired to go over it with you tonight. It's been an exhausting day.

Oh, the good news is, Lisa is back and has some scoop on Caruso, too."

"I can't wait to hear the news. What time do you think you'll be here tomorrow?"

"Barring delays, early afternoon. I'll text if we experience any significant delays."

"Okay, sweetie, get a nice shower and curl up in the bed. I can't wait to share this huge garden tub when you get here."

"Sounds great, Blair. I can't wait to see you." Tally paused. "Oh, hey, wait. Do you have any pull with Director Lewis in Jackson? Could you maybe arrange for Jamie Carson to spend a few days with us in Texas? Especially since one of the victims was a resident of his state?"

"I've met him before. I'll give him a call and see what I can do. We could use a chauffeur for a few days. The agent here offered or stated she could get a car for us, but if Jamie stays, he can drive us."

"That's what I was thinking. Jamie is young and may benefit from time spent with us. He already idolizes you." Tally chuckled.

Blair smiled at the sound of Tally's laughter. "Okay, I'll see what I can do. Can't wait to see you. Sweet dreams."

"Goodnight, Blair. I love you."

"I love you too. Be safe tomorrow."

Tally plugged her phone into the charger and picked up her sleep clothes. The shower was relaxing, and when she slipped under the covers, she picked up her notepad and reviewed her notes. Tally's eyes grew heavy, and after jotting a few more notes, she turned out the light.

†

Blair finished her night routine and prepared to climb into the bed. Her notes on Caruso were fanned out across the bed. She gathered them into a file and placed it on her desk.

†

Caruso stretched out on his cot and smiled. He read the encrypted letter from Bobby and smiled as he knew his plan was in place. Bobby had turned into a gem, not the usual serial killer wannabe that had written him so often. Bobby was intelligent and quickly learned to decipher Casper's writings. He smiled and tucked the letter into the box that held his correspondence and legal documents. Tomorrow was the beginning of his last hurrah, and he wanted to be well rested. Casper knew Blair Cooper was intelligent, and he would have to work hard to stay a step ahead of her. He was up to the task and curled up in his sheets to fall asleep.

†

Tally stretched as she sat up in bed. The covers were barely disturbed from her night's sleep. She didn't remember dreaming either, which was highly unusual for her. She felt well-rested as she climbed from the bed, stripped, and packed her sleep clothes in her bag. Tally showered and dressed before heading to breakfast. She stopped at the front desk to return her key and then requested a cooked-to-order breakfast. She was halfway through her meal when Jamie arrived.

"Sorry, I couldn't wait."

"No problem. That omelet looks delicious."

"It is delicious," Tally replied.

Jamie walked over to the breakfast counter and ordered. He returned with a bowl of fresh fruit to snack on while he waited on breakfast. Tally had just finished her juice. "Do you want more apple juice?"

"Yes, that would be great. Thank you."

Jamie returned with a fresh glass of apple juice for them both. "Don't stop eating. I'll catch up quick," he grinned. "I love breakfast."

"I can eat it any time of the day," Tally admitted.

"Me, too. I eat it a lot for dinner."

"I've been known to do that on occasion," Tally said as she took a bite.

Tally's phone pinged with a text. *Tell Jamie he gets to spend the week with us.*

Thanks. Jamie will be excited. See you soon. Love you.

Tally looked up at Jamie, who had just taken a bite of melon. She decided she'd better allow him to swallow before she shared the news. He saw her grinning.

"What? Did I spill something already?" he asked.

"That was Agent Cooper. You get to spend the week with us," Tally smiled.

"Alright," he said a bit loudly.

Tally smiled at his exuberance. "You will be our escort in Texas, but Director Lewis said you have to be back in the office Monday."

"I'll take any time I can get with you two," he replied.

†

Blair met Linda in the lobby, and they drove out to the Huntsville Penitentiary.

"That's quite an ominous building," Blair said.

"It's seen more than its fair share of evil during its history. Some of the worst criminals in American history have passed through these gates. Caruso is just another notch in the bedpost. The state of Texas will breathe a sigh of relief after December twelfth."

"I was surprised when he reached out to us. I know there's not an ounce of remorse in him, so I think he's grasping his last opportunity to be in the limelight."

"If he asks to be a part of locating the victims, do you believe he will be allowed to leave the prison?" Linda asked.

"I will make it clear up front that's not a possibility," Blair replied.

Linda shut off the vehicle. "I know we can prevent him from escaping, but I can't guarantee we could defend his safety if word got out, he was outside these prison walls. Even if it were to be to assist in locating remains."

"I can understand that. If I were a family member of one of his victims and had a chance for revenge, I might be tempted."

"I have a gun safe in my interior fender well if you'd like to leave your sidearm. You won't have to go through the hassle inside if you do."

"Thanks, I won't be needing it inside anyhow." Blair opened the door and stepped out into a humid Texas morning. She removed her gun and handed it to Linda as she walked to the rear of the vehicle.

Linda secured their weapons, and they began the task of clearing the checkpoints into the prison.

When they were settled into the conference room, Warden Foster came in to introduce himself.

"Very pleased to meet you, ladies," he said with a deep Texas drawl. "I don't envy you having to spend time with Caruso this week. Honestly, I can't wait until that arrogant bastard departs this place."

Blair nodded. "I'm sure there are plenty who share that sentiment. I'm only here to gather whatever information we can on other victims so we can give families some closure, and closeout open cases."

"Let me know if there is anything else you need," the warden said.

"My partner, Tally Rainwater, and her escort, Agent Jamie Carson, will be arriving around noon. Will you see that entry is expedited for them?"

"That won't be a problem." The warden left the room, and Linda busied herself setting up the video camera.

"Our guest of honor should be arriving soon. Try to have minimal contact with him. As soon as Tally arrives, I'm going to ask Jamie to replace you. He will be less of a distraction to Caruso. You can still monitor from the outer room if you choose."

Linda nodded. "Not a problem. I understand, but I would like to monitor if that's okay."

"How would you feel if you and Jamie do some legwork for us. Once he starts revealing locations, I'd like you to go to the spots to determine if he's telling the truth."

"That shouldn't be a problem. Hopefully, it won't be a wild goose chase."

Blair smiled at Linda. "It may not be easy to locate the victims, but I think he's given enough thought to this to know he has to give up at least a few to keep us here. That's what it's all about for him. Seeing his name in the media one last time." She gave Linda a card with her cell number on the back. "You can text me on this number if you've recovered anything or have questions. I will have my phone on silent, but I'll feel the vibrations. Anything we can do to limit the attention he gets, the better."

†

A few minutes later, a knock sounded on the door, and it swung open. Casper Caruso entered the room, followed closely by a guard. The guard removed the shackles from Caruso's legs and secured his wrist cuffs to the table.

"I'll be right outside if you need anything. I'll take him back to his cell for lunch at eleven," the guard said. "What time would you like me to bring him back?"

"One thirty will be fine. It will give us time for a lunch break as well."

"Yes, ma'am," the guard replied and stepped out of the room.

Blair glanced at Caruso. He wanted her to know he was studying Linda.

He spent several long seconds looking at Linda before he turned his attention to Blair.

"It's so good to see you again, Agent Cooper. The company you keep these days sure is a lot prettier," he said, nodding his head toward Linda. "Where's the freak?"

"If you are referring to Ms. Rainwater, she'll be here later. If you plan on addressing her in that manner, I'll just ask her to stay away. She had a side trip to make before arriving here. I can't say that you've gotten any prettier."

"The spa options are rather limited here," Caruso grinned. "Tanning options are out, too, since my hour of freedom is at two in the morning. Not much chance of sunshine then." He smiled. "I'll play nice with her."

"You won't have to worry about freedom soon." Blair looked directly into his blue eyes for any signs of a reaction.

Caruso chuckled. "I can see you haven't changed much, Agent Cooper. You still cut straight to the bone."

"I've got no time for games. Killers like you keep crawling out from under rocks, so that keeps me busy." Blair saw Linda's reflection in the glass window and saw she was covering her mouth to prevent a laugh. She would have to address this later. Caruso didn't miss the action, though.

"Your pretty little blonde Barbie doll thought that was funny," Caruso chuckled. "I guess she's never seen the photos of what I do to pretty little things like her after I'm done with them."

"I'm sure she's seen things just as bad, probably worse," Blair challenged him.

"Could be. I get letters all the time from other prospects looking to make a name for themselves. Most are just juvenile thugs, but every now and then a gem comes along."

"I'm sure I will be meeting them one day," Blair said.

"That's always a possibility." Caruso grinned and leaned forward. "I'm sure you'll track them down just like you did me. Eventually."

"I was curious why you wanted to come clean on a few more victims. That doesn't seem your style at all."

"Maybe the media will give me a welcome send off if you can locate the other victims. One final attempt to show them I'm not the monster I'm portrayed to be."

It was Blair's turn to laugh. "I don't think a little bit of coverage on old news will get the media to change their opinion of you."

"Only time will tell." He relaxed back into his seat.

"Well, this was your request, so let's get to it. Let's set some ground rules first." Blair looked at him. "First, any sign of a wild goose chase, and we end the search for new victims, and nothing is released to the press."

"A few won't be all that easy to find, but I'll get you as close as I can. I've even drawn out a few little maps for you for nine of them. The tenth has long been devoured by the ocean. She was my first, and in my haste for enjoyment, I forgot that there could be no confirmation without a body or remains."

"A rookie's mistake." Blair shrugged. "It happens to the best of them."

"Her name was Wanda Harrison, a bartender down in Beaumont. She thought the tips I was giving her were enough to show that I had money. When I told her, I had a boat docked in the marina, she jumped at the chance to spend the weekend with me."

"Any date that you can remember?" Blair asked.

Caruso gave her a wicked grin. "You know we never forget our firsts. Any of them for that matter." He appeared to be thinking for a few seconds. "The two of us left the Galveston Harbor on Saturday, October second, in two thousand and five. Only one of us returned on the third. Ironically, I sectioned her up and fed her to some sharks within sight of one of the oil platforms I used to work on." He grinned. "I had been chumming the water for fish, and when the sharks began showing up, I just couldn't resist watching them feed."

Blair made notes on the victim with as little emotional response as she could muster. She resisted asking the obvious question of whether Wanda had already been dead when she was fed to the sharks, but that detail really didn't matter, since it was just his story. Blair would have to confirm a missing person report for the woman before more action could be taken.

He chuckled. "Don't you want to know more about that one?"

Blair shook her head nonchalantly. "You were right. Since there are no remains to recover, we can't confirm her as a victim. Do you have any evidence to prove she was with you?"

"Only if you can find the lucky sonofabitch that got to buy my boat for pennies on the dollar after my incarceration. In the sleeping quarters, there is a small hidden storage compartment under the bed. You can find several Polaroid pics I snapped as she was sunbathing and a gold chain she wore on her wrist. If not, you can chalk that one up as history."

"Did you have a rental slot for the boat? We would need more information on where it was stored to be able to track it down."

"I had a regular slip in Galveston for years. The harbor authority could probably help with that information. I'm sure it was auctioned off for non-payment of slip rental."

"Was it a nice boat?" Blair asked.

Caruso sighed. "She was a beauty. I bought her while I was working offshore. The top of the line is the only way to go. She set me back a pretty penny, but she was worth the expense."

"What was her name?" Blair asked.

"The Castaway," he answered.

"Interesting name. Why that one?" she asked.

"My name was often mispronounced as Crusoe, like Robinson Crusoe, who has always been one of my favorite stories."

"Did you read all the versions or just Defoe's? Blair asked.

Caruso's brow shot up in surprise. "You know the original? I'm impressed, Agent Cooper. There have been so many spinoffs to the original story, the brilliance of Defoe was lost."

"The advent of cinematography changed many original stories for the sake of entertainment."

"That's so very true. Both have merits, but the original story is a masterpiece."

Blair placed her pen back on the table. "We only have a few minutes before it will be time for your meal. Do you wish to say more or want to wait until we resume?"

"I'll go now, I have the next two mapped out for you. No wild goose chases. I promise."

"I will see you after lunch." Blair waited until he left the room to call Linda over to the table. "Are you ready to do some research?"

"The boat?"

"Yes, let's grab a quick sandwich, and you can set up my laptop and begin your searching. I'd start with the victim first, to see if she's genuinely a missing person or a figment of his imagination. If we can't determine she is real, there's no need to track down the boat."

"That makes sense." She smiled. "Are you up for some brisket?"

"I've been told I must try it," Blair said, returning her smile. "Let me send a quick text to Tally to see where they are."

"Do we need to lock up here?" Linda asked.

"No, I think things are pretty safe here. We can check with the warden on the way out."

Her phone pinged as they left the room. *Thirty minutes out.*

Hungry? Blair asked.

Starving.

"Where are we going?" she asked Linda.

Linda gave her the name of the restaurant, which she texted to Tally. *See you soon.*

After a quick stop at the Warden's office, they were given a key to the conference room. "I'll have someone lock it for you. Enjoy some good brisket," he told them.

"Is brisket the most famous food in Texas?" Blair asked.

Linda chuckled and nodded. "Followed closely by chicken-fried steak."

"Another first to add to my list then," Blair said.

"The place right across from the hotel, the Farmhouse, is well known for theirs. Better bo hungry, though. The portions are huge."

"Now you're making my mouth water. Brisket first, I'm buying."

†

When they arrived at the restaurant, they got a table for four. Blair ordered sweet tea for Tally and sent a text to ask what Jamie would like to drink.

Sweet tea for both of us. Tally answered.

Both up for trying the brisket?

Sure, go ahead and order, we'll be there in just a few minutes.

Done, Blair replied. "This place smells heavenly. If the food tastes half as good as it smells, it'll be great."

"If you don't like it, I'll buy," Linda said.

"That's confidence." Blair chuckled.

†

Blair smiled when she saw Tally and Jamie enter. She waved them over and made the introductions. Jamie sat next to Linda as Tally took the seat beside Blair.

"I'm glad you two made it in time for lunch. We're just a few minutes away from the prison, and we don't resume with Caruso until one-thirty."

"How's it going with him so far?" Jamie asked.

"He's revealed the first victim, but we won't be able to confirm the claim. We do have some evidence to possibly track down. If we're successful with that, we can at least update any family members we can find. No remains to recover, though."

Tally cocked her head. "Destroyed?"

"Worse, but I don't think we need to discuss it here," Blair said.

"He sounds like he's been cooperative," Jamie said.

"So far, yes. Caruso claims to have some maps drawn up for us. If he does, I want you and Linda to do some fieldwork and see if we can recover the victims. Linda has jurisdiction, so she'll need to call in the locals."

"Has he shown you a list of names yet?" Tally asked.

"No, not yet," Blair answered. "Why?"

"I wanted to see if he listed the young woman from Mississippi. If not, he's not giving you all his victims."

"I'll press him for the others when we return," Blair replied. "He seemed disappointed when you weren't with me this morning."

"I don't look forward to looking into those cold eyes again," Tally said.

"He's much calmer than I expected. He's either on some effective meds, or he's resigned himself to his fate."

"He did seem more reserved than I anticipated after reading about him," Linda agreed.

The waitress brought plates of food to the table, and they started the meal. Tally's eyes landed on the large stack of onion rings on Blair's plate. "You know I have to try those, right?" She pointed her fork at the fried onions.

"I was wondering how long it would take you to notice." Blair swapped plates with Tally. "I knew you couldn't resist those when I saw them on someone's plate."

Jamie took a drink and smiled at Blair. "Thanks for getting the Director to allow me to spend the week here."

"Have no fear, we are going to get our money's worth out of you," Blair replied as she waved her knife in the air. "He made me promise to work you hard."

Jamie grinned. "I'm not scared of hard work."

"That's exactly what Director Lewis said. I think he likes you just a bit."

"That's good to know." Jamie took another bite of food. "This is really good."

"Thank Linda. It was her suggestion," Blair told him.

He smiled sweetly to her. "This is fantastic. Thanks."

"Just wait til you get to dinner tonight." She grinned back at him.

Tally looked at Blair. "You've already got dinner planned?"

Blair nodded. "We're trying Texas' second-most iconic food. Chicken-fried steak."

CHAPTER SIX

When they returned to the prison, Blair got her laptop set up for Linda, and Jamie used his to begin researching the identity of the first victim. Blair had them arranged in a monitoring room just outside the conference room.

"Remember, once Caruso comes back into the room, you should only text. Tally will be monitoring my phone."

"I'll also text if there are additional clues he gives us," Tally said. "You can be looking up stuff while we interview him. If he gives us bad information, we'll know immediately. The names will be the first thing to search."

"Got it," Jamie said.

"I'll start the recording once we get settled in," Tally told Blair.

"We've got a few minutes, so let me know if you get any hits," Blair said and returned to the conference room.

"Good luck, you two," Tally said and followed Blair.

When they were settled in the conference room, Tally turned to Blair. "Other than starting the recording, what do you want me to do?"

"Just listen to see if you pick up on anything I may miss. If you need further clarification, ask Caruso your questions. Let's not bring up your trip to Mississippi until we have a chance to discuss it."

"Okay, don't forget to ask him for the list, please," Tally replied.

Blair nodded. "Thanks for the reminder."

Tally pulled out her notebook and turned to a fresh page.

†

A few minutes later, the soft knock preceded the door opening, and Caruso was led back into the room. When he was cuffed to the table, Tally stood to start the camera.

Caruso stared at her with his cold blue eyes. "It's lovely to see you again, Ms. Rainwater, and have a chance for a formal introduction. I've followed your work closely. Quite impressive."

"It appears you had been busy as well," Tally replied.

"Well, yes, that's why we're here today, isn't it?" He grinned at Blair. "I hope you enjoyed your brisket. I'm sure it was much tastier than the mystery meat patty we had."

"It was quite good," Blair said. "We're going for chicken-fried steak tonight."

"Dear Lord, you're hitting all my favorites. That will be my request for my last meal."

"I can't make a promise, but if the warden agrees when we get done here, I'll bring you whatever you want for a going-away lunch. If we're successful." She pushed a piece of paper and a pencil toward him. "The next thing we need from you is a list of your ten victims, so we can start some research."

"There's no need for that. I already have it for you," Caruso said. He opened the small Bible and took out the list. He handed it over to Blair. "Can we negotiate dessert as well?"

"I'd bet you want banana pudding," Tally said. "It was incredible today."

"Now you're teasing me, little missy. That's my favorite."

Tally copied the names onto her notepad and then left the room with her list. She was pleased to see *Alice Carmichael*, the young woman from Mississippi, on the roster near the end. She took the slip of paper to Jamie. "Here's the list of victims to start tracking down."

"We have confirmed the Galveston victim is a missing person. Linda is trying to track down the boat now," Jamie said.

"Great job, you two. Keep the good news coming." Tally left the room.

†

"That's a good start," Blair said as Tally entered the room and nodded to Blair.

Tally returned to her seat and studied the names staring up at her. "We know Wanda is a real person, but what about some of these other names?" Tally asked. "Locations and dates would be helpful. Are they all located in Texas?"

"My goodness, you're full of questions all of a sudden," Caruso replied. "All but two are in Texas. Alice Carmichael was a sweet little thing from Mississippi, and Shavon Caire was from Baton Rouge. Her body has already been recovered, but her case is unsolved."

"How do you know her body has been recovered?" Blair asked.

"She was located before my incarceration, but those crazy Cajuns never had a clue she could be linked to me. I also get library privileges once in a while, and I follow some cases on the Internet. I have to be cautious to erase my cookies, so the brilliant officers here can't trace me. Not that they would be so inclined." He chuckled. "If it's not about the Cowboys or Astros, they could care less about the Internet." He clicked his tongue over his teeth. "Shameful, really. A teenager could track some of these dummies activity on the internet with their eyes closed."

Blair made a mental note of that comment to share with the warden as well as her director. That could be useful in tracking some prison data in the future.

Blair chuckled. "I know, the technology young kids can zip through these days is impressive. I have a hard time setting up a new phone."

"Society has become enslaved to technology. I'd have lost my teeth if I brought a cell phone to the dinner table." Caruso laughed.

Blair nodded. "That is so true. It's scary what all you can do with phones and the Internet."

"I've only got until four today, so I guess we'd better get back to it," Caruso said. "So, you know Caire, and now you can link me to her. I'd learned my lesson after Wanda about leaving a body intact, so I made her easy to find. Or so I thought. I left her in the trunk of her car at Death Valley after an LSU football game on November twenty-fifth, two thousand and five. Very close game with Arkansas, but the Tigers pulled out a win. It was several days before they thought to check out the abandoned car. Guess that's not that uncommon during football season."

"You have a good memory," Blair commented.

"Some men have sports trophies to gloat on for years. Those sixteen dates are all I have."

"So far, you have given us two that are easy enough to track. What is something to prove you killed Caire? Something no one else would know about?"

"Her family and maybe others she had been intimate with would know that she had a heart-shaped birthmark on her pelvis. I kept our ticket stubs from the game, but I'm sure they were tossed out by my landlord years ago."

Blair noticed him glance up at the clock. "I know we don't have much more time today. Shift change will be happening soon."

Caruso opened up his Bible and handed Blair two more slips of paper. "These are as close as I can remember. I don't know if either has been recovered, but this is where I left them and the dates. If you get those young agents on the ball, they might start the searches tonight."

Blair handed the two maps to Tally. "Ask Linda to make several copies, please."

Tally nodded and left the room.

"Don't those eyes freak you out just a bit?" Caruso asked when Tally stepped out.

"No, I've become very accustomed to them. Tally is very talented," Blair responded.

"Oh, I bet she is," Caruso chuckled.

"Now, now, you promised to be nice," Blair reminded him. "So, what's good with chicken-fried steak?"

Caruso smiled at her. "Mashed potatoes and gravy, maybe some sweet corn or green beans."

"I don't think I can do more beans. I had baked beans with the brisket, and they are killing me." Blair chuckled.

"They used to give me fits, too, but oh man, did I love them."

Tally slipped back into the room behind the officer.

"Time to go," he said gruffly.

"Same time tomorrow?" Caruso asked.

"We'll be here," Blair said.

"Enjoy that chicken-fried," he said as he was led out of the room.

"We will," Blair said. She turned to Tally. "Ask Linda and Jamie to join us briefly."

When they entered the room, Blair went into action. "Linda, I'd like you and Jamie to track down information on these two new cases in Texas. I'll work on the woman from Louisiana. Tally, I'd like you to take the tape from today and review it to see if you pick up anything. I have a player in the hotel. We need to get Jamie a room, and see if they have a room we can use."

"I can handle that while you get packed up," Linda offered.

"Good deal," Blair said.

†

"Let me take your bags up for you," Jamie said to Tally when they pulled up.

"I don't think you need to," Tally said as she motioned to the porter coming with a cart.

"You can take those to Room 223," Blair said as she handed him a tip. "We've got a conference room downstairs," she told Tally and Jamie. "Jamie, you can get checked in and grab your bags later."

"Yes, ma'am," he said and handed the keys to the valet.

"We've got work to do." Tally smiled at him. "I'm going up to the room to review today's tape, and then I'll join you."

"See you soon." Blair smiled at her.

†

They settled into the conference room and began making phone calls. It wasn't long before both Jamie and Linda reported local authorities were sent a copy of the maps Caruso provided and were sending teams out to investigate. Blair had similar success with Baton Rouge. The lead detective was very appreciative of her information. He confirmed the presence of the birthmark and other information Caruso had provided.

"I'm so happy to finally be able to close that case. It's haunted me for years. The family will be glad to hear Caruso

111

will be executed soon for his crimes. It only saddens me that her dad has passed without knowing there was justice for his baby."

"That's a tough one. I don't envy you the task of informing the family, but maybe they can gain some sense of closure," Blair replied.

The call to Galveston also enabled the detectives to close a case. They didn't see a need to follow up on the boat since Wanda had no relatives listed, and Caruso was already scheduled for execution. Blair was disappointed in the response. She was not one to leave any evidence undiscovered, but she reckoned they didn't have the manpower to follow up the lead.

When Tally joined them, she took a seat beside Blair and got an update on their calls.

"With everything we learned today, we are halfway through his list. I really thought he would be more challenging."

Blair nodded. "We aren't at the finish line yet. You can bet he's saving the best for last. I think we've done all we can until we hear back from the local crews. Let's freshen up a bit and go try that chicken-fried."

Jamie smiled at Linda. "Will you be joining us?"

She returned his smile. "I don't mind if I do."

"Can you also point me to a mall or someplace I can pick up a few more shirts?"

"We can ride together. After dinner, we can drop these two back here, and I'll take you for shirts."

"Thank you for not making us tag along." Blair chuckled. "We'll be back down in ten. Do we need a reservation?" Blair asked Linda.

"I'll get us one, just in case. I'll pull the car around and meet you in a few." Linda pulled out her phone and started walking through the lobby.

Tally noticed Jamie following her with his eyes. "She is attractive."

When Jamie realized he'd been busted, he blushed. "Yeah, I'd have to agree."

Blair couldn't resist the opportunity to tease the young man. "Come along, Romeo. You can grab your bag from our room and powder your nose before we eat."

†

Blair closed the door behind Jamie and rushed across the room to take Tally in her arms. "I know it was only one night, but I missed you." She kissed her sweetly.

"I missed you, too," Tally replied after the kiss.

Blair pointed at the large garden tub. "You and I have a date with some French Vanilla bubble bath when we get back tonight."

"That sounds fantastic. It's huge." Tally grinned.

"I want to hear all about your trip to Mississippi," Blair said. "You sounded intrigued on the phone."

"It was an exciting trip, and I met a highly intelligent young woman in the process."

"Oh, should I be jealous?" Blair feigned hurt.

"No, Blair, you know my heart is all yours. Besides, she has a girlfriend already." She chuckled.

"I think our young friends may have some mutual attraction going on, too," Blair said. "Jamie nearly drools every time he looks Linda's way."

"Uh, huh, I noticed that, too," Tally replied. "At least they would understand the stressors of the job if they had a relationship. It can be stressful on a relationship if you have to worry about your loved one coming home safe every night. Also, the horrible things we often see on cases can take a toll on the human psyche as well."

"Do you feel stressed?" Blair asked.

"Not usually because I am normally with you, but I'll admit I worry when we're apart."

"I promise to always return safely to you." Blair kissed her again. "Let's go eat."

†

Tally was surprised that chicken-fried steak was not actually chicken, but she enjoyed the meal. "They either need bigger plates or smaller portions." She laughed as she took a bite. "This is delicious."

"I think the portions are just fine," Jamie said as he scooped up the last bite of his mashed potatoes.

"Will you please have some of mine then?" Tally asked. She cut a large section and offered it to him.

"Well, I'd hate to see it go to waste." He grinned.

"Enjoy," Blair told him. "Mine is going into the mini-fridge in my room."

Tally was amazed that Jamie had room for dessert, but he did, and she and Blair split a bowl of banana pudding.

"I do believe I am sufficiently stuffed," Tally said, and she pushed the container to Blair for the last bite. "I'm also glad I don't have to waddle through a mall tonight, too."

"I had forgotten about that. Oh, well, it'll give us a chance to walk off some calories." Jamie grinned at Linda.

†

Once they were dropped at the hotel and safely tucked away in their room, Blair and Tally got undressed. Blair started drawing a bath and portioned out some bubble bath.

"This is going to feel so good." She stepped into the water and held a hand to Tally for support.

Tally sat between Blair's legs and leaned back onto her chest. "This is heavenly," she purred. The warm water swirled around her body once Blair activated the jets.

Blair wrapped her arms around Tally's waist. "Tell me about Mississippi, please."

Tally relaxed in Blair's arms. "You remember me telling you about a young woman digging up some strange knives?"

"Yes, I do," Blair answered.

"Her name is Haley, and she's an archeology student at Mississippi State. Her class had been working on a dig site near a Natchez tribe village. She remained behind to dig while her classmates took advantage of the long weekend to travel to New Orleans to party."

"That's a dedicated student that would pass on a chance to hit Bourbon Street." Blair chuckled.

"She's extremely serious about her calling. Haley told me she was compelled to dig at one particular site, and that's where she uncovered the ceremonial knives." Tally paused for a breath. "That's also where she was going when she saw an apparition of Alice and followed it into the woods to discover the remains."

"You really think it was a ghost?" Blair asked.

"Yes, I do. There was a lot of residual energy at both sites, not all good either. I was relieved when Lisa arrived and helped me identify Caruso as the killer."

"I'm glad she finally decided to return. I know you were worried." Blair said.

"One day, Lisa will leave me, but hopefully no time soon." Tally sighed. "After beating and raping her repeatedly, Caruso took Alice into the woods and tied her to an oak tree. I could feel her pain as the bark bit into her skin as she tried to struggle against her bindings to no avail. I heard his evil laugh as he opened a straight razor and slashed her throat."

Blair's arms tightened around Tally. "That must have been horrible to watch."

"It's never easy, especially when the victim is so young with so much life ahead of her. At least she can be at peace now, and her family has her remains to place in a grave." She paused again, thinking of the young woman's family. "When I had seen all I could, I asked Haley to take me back to her dig site. We talked about the knives she uncovered, and I asked her to retrieve them for me. I had seen two young Native American women, who I felt were lovers. When Haley placed the knives in my hands, the vision returned."

"It's so amazing how objects can trigger your visions."

"It really helps to have something close to them to center my energy on. The two young women were daughters of the primary chiefs of the tribe. The War Chief was killed in battle, and as customary, a human was sacrificed to accompany him in the afterlife. The two lovers knew their lives together would never be accepted, so they took it upon themselves to sacrifice their youth to be together forever."

Blair nuzzled into Tally's neck. "You go from the tragic to the romantic in a matter of minutes. At least you ended the trip on a positive note."

"Yes. I told Haley she would uncover them entwined in one another's arms, positioned just as they had died. Because their sacrifice was not approved, they were buried there instead of at the Emerald Mound. It didn't matter, though. They were to spend eternity together forever."

"How do you feel about Alice's name being on his list?"

"It confirms he is telling us the truth, or at least a portion of it. I think he may have other victims beyond the ten. I'd like to hear his details of killing Alice to confirm what I saw in my vision."

"What makes you believe he may have more victims?" Blair asked.

"According to his dates, his killing cycle was barely a month. If he started in two thousand and five at barely a month apart, I'd say chances are there were periods when his kills grew much closer as his need to dominate and feel the power over life grew."

"That is a probable assumption. I feel like we will be fortunate to receive ten. Caruso may not remember any others, or maybe he will let something slip that you can recover."

"Maybe so," Tally replied.

Blair could hear the relaxed quality in Tally's voice. She knew the emotional toll Tally's visions took on her strength, sometimes lasting for days. "Are you ready to run through a shower to get these bubbles rinsed off and snuggle the night away?"

"That sounds perfect," Tally replied. She turned in Blair's arms and kissed her deeply.

†

Once they had settled between the sheets, Tally turned to Blair. "I love you so much."

"I know," Blair smiled. "I love you too. Maybe after we get done here, we can try for another vacation. I hear Maine has horrible cellphone reception."

"I've never been to Maine," Tally answered. "There are many places I've never been, but Blair Cooper, I will follow you anywhere."

"I think the Director owes us a favor for cutting our trip short." Blair kissed Tally. "Goodnight, my love."

CHAPTER SEVEN

Blair saw the scowl on Tally's face. "Are you okay?"

"Something feels off today," Tally said when they finished breakfast.

"Do you know what it is?" Blair asked her partner.

Tally shook her head. "No, I wish I could pinpoint it, but I can't."

When they walked outside, Blair could see a bank of dark clouds to the south. She looked at Tally, who was also watching them roll in.

"I can smell the rain in the air mixed with sulfur," Tally said.

"If the storm rolls in while we're at the prison, I want you to go to the other room. Okay?" Blair suggested.

"Yes, I agree that it would be a good idea. I don't want to be a distraction to either of you on what should be our last day with Caruso."

"Let me know if you sense something I need to be aware of immediately. Hopefully, it's just the storm rolling in that has you on edge."

Tally forced a smile. "I hope so, too."

"Are you ladies ready to beat this rain?" Jamie said as he came bouncing out of the hotel.

"Let's do this. The sooner we get done, the sooner we can head for home," Blair responded. "Let's meet up with Linda to focus on our game plan for the day."

The mention of Linda's name brought a smile to Jamie's face. Neither Tally nor Blair missed the expression.

"You like her, don't you?" Tally teased. She watched the blush rise up his freshly shaved face.

"What's not to like? She's beautiful, intelligent, and down to earth."

"Maybe you should ask her out for tomorrow night?" Tally suggested. "Unless Caruso has some stall tactic planned, we should be done here today."

"I had that very thought in mind. I've got the weekend before I need to head back to Mississippi."

"Make the most of it." Blair grinned at him as he held their doors open.

†

Tally frowned as they arrived at the prison. The dark clouds appeared to hover over the building, making it feel

120

even more ominous. Blair handed Jamie her sidearm to store in the safe, and they walked to the entrance.

Linda was waiting in the lobby, and she beamed when she saw them. Tally grinned. She doubted that beautiful smile was for anyone but Jamie. They did make a handsome couple.

After going through security, they met in the conference room.

"If everything goes as smoothly as yesterday, I hope we can finish up today," Blair announced. "He's been forthright with us so far, so I have no reason to think that won't continue."

Linda cocked her head at Blair. "I'm still shocked by how candid he's being. Makes me concerned he is up to something devious."

Blair looked at Linda. "Tally has a sense something is off too, so let's stay on our toes."

"Do you want us in the outer room to start?" Jamie asked.

"Yes. If this storm rolls in, Tally will join you. Electrical storms activate her visions, and I want her safe from Caruso."

"We'll make sure she stays safe," Linda promised.

†

When Caruso entered the room, he smiled at Blair and Tally. "Good morning, ladies. I hope you rested well last night."

"I slept like a rock after the chicken-fried steak and banana pudding," Blair told him. "Is that what you still want to eat?"

"That sounds yummy. I can hardly wait. I guess we'd better get started then. I have the rest mapped out for you, but there is one we need to discuss more in-depth" He held back one piece of paper. "You can give these four to your students, but this one is for us." Caruso pushed four pieces of paper across to Blair.

Blair looked over the four sheets of paper. She smiled when she saw Alice Carmichael on the second sheet. She pulled that one out and handed the remaining three to Tally, who took them to Jamie. When Tally returned to her seat, Blair picked up the paper with Alice's name. "Tell me about this one? Why someone so far away?"

"I was actually returning from Florida. I went to Destin to go deep-sea fishing. That was a fantastic trip. I caught a jumbo grouper on that trip. What a challenge to land that monster." He grinned at Blair. "Do you fish?"

"I've been known to on occasion. I prefer fresh water though," Blair replied.

"Yeah, any kind of fishing or hunting is good." He looked at Blair. "Okay, back to work. I stopped in some little podunk town along I-10 in Mississippi and saw her alone in a parking lot."

Blair looked at the date. "Not long after Wanda or Shavon. Was Alice number three for you?"

"Three. After that, they seemed to come faster and faster. I don't know if I was becoming a better hunter, or the women were just so careless."

122

Blair scoffed. "I don't think it was careless. Nobody had linked you to any deaths yet, so they had no idea you were out there."

"Maybe so. Alice was a pretty little thing, but she tried her best to put up a fight. I was breathing hard when the gas finally put her out." He grinned at Tally. "She was still a virgin, too. Pure as the driven snow. I think she was the first I ever experienced, so tight and firm." He grinned as he watched Tally recoil away from the table.

The storm finally hit, and the lights flickered in the room. "Don't worry, you won't be left in the dark with me," Caruso taunted Tally when the emergency lights came on. "The generator will kick on in fifteen seconds if we lose power."

Tally could feel the hairs on her arms standing up. The electrical storm had arrived. She silently counted after the first bolt of lightning until the boom of thunder arrived. Very close. "I'll be back in a bit," Tally told Blair as she stood and left the room.

"What's the matter? She scared of a little storm?" Caruso asked Blair. His wicked grin faded when Blair calmly said, "She was hit by lightning when she was young."

"Damn, that had to hurt. I'm glad I've got a lethal injection to look forward to instead of the electric chair. I bet riding the pine is one hell of a painful way to go."

"It's definitely not a pretty sight," Blair nodded.

Caruso leaned forward. "You've seen one?"

"Two actually," Blair replied. "I can only imagine the stench in the room."

"If I sent you an invitation, would you attend my execution?" Caruso asked.

"I don't know. It would depend on what's going on at the time," Blair answered him honestly. "I'd like to for the victims who had no one there for them, but we'll have to see."

The lights came back on without the generator. "Tell me more about Alice."

"I had my way with her for two days in my Chevy van. When she started to look weak, I was done. I found a nice secluded spot in the woods far away from town and put a bullet to her head."

†

"That sonofabitch is lying," Tally said in the outer room. She started to stand just as she heard Blair's calm voice.

"Wait," Jamie said.

Tally returned to her seat when she felt her vision blur. She closed her eyes and waited.

†

"I'm disappointed in you, Casper. Up to now, you have been relatively honest and cooperative. Why the change?"

"What do you mean?" Caruso looked startled.

"I know for a fact that she wasn't shot. So, are you lying, or was Alice Carmichael not your work?"

Caruso's chuckle sounded evil. "Oh, she was definitely one of mine. I was just testing you."

"So, let's get back on track with the truth." Blair challenged him.

"I take it her body has been recovered, or you wouldn't know that."

Blair stared into his cold blue eyes. "I know more than that. I can recite word for word the last thing you said to her, but I'd still like to hear your version."

"How could you? Oh, wait, Ms. Rainwater? Is that why she was late in joining our party?"

Blair nodded and waited for him to continue.

Caruso laughed and sat back in his chair. "When I tired of her, I dressed her in her raggedy-ass clothes. I drove until I found a thick plot of woods. It didn't look like anyone had been in the area for ages. Near the trail, it was swampy, so I didn't think even hunters would venture that way."

"You were right, for almost fifteen years," Blair confirmed.

"I carried her to a large oak tree and used a rope to bind her. When she came around from the drugs, her eyes grew wide with terror. She recognized this was her end."

"So, no quick bullet to the head," Blair prompted.

"Naw, that would have been too easy. I considered leaving her alive to see if Alice could manage to escape. She was a real fighter, probably the toughest of any of them. In the end, though, I couldn't stand the suspense. I pulled a straight razor from my pocket and slit her throat."

"That's much better," Blair said.

"What was the last thing I said to her?" Caruso asked.

Blair checked her notes, even though she hadn't needed to. "You told her she was one fine piece of ass."

His eyes shot towards the door where Tally had exited. "Damn, she is good."

"She's been watching you for a couple of weeks now," Blair tossed out. Inwardly she was extremely pleased to see the shocked look on his face.

"You have been in several of her visions, but it wasn't until recently that she figured out who you were."

†

Casper felt the hairs on the back of his neck rise. *So, it hadn't been my imagination when I felt like someone was watching me. The freak was spying on me. No worries. I've got something planned for her that will rock her world. I bet you don't know a thing about that.* He smiled at Blair. *Oh, what I have planned for you. It's epic.*

†

Tally settled back into her seat and let the vision begin to flow. She blocked out all sound and concentrated on the images in front of her eyes. Caruso was with a young red-haired woman. Strangely enough, they were at a restaurant, eating dinner. The shadows from the candlelight flickered across the young woman's face as she looked at Caruso. She couldn't hide the surprise on her face when he pulled out a small velvet box and opened it. Caruso was proposing to her. Tally watched her nod, and Caruso placed the ring on her finger. Tally noted how young he looked in the vision.

When the scene shifted, it showed Caruso working on an oil platform out in the Gulf. He was covered in sweat and grime. It was evident to Tally that he had been working hard. The wind was blowing along with a heavy rain as the men appeared to be evacuating the platform. Caruso drove in the pouring rain to make it home. Tally watched as he pulled into his neighborhood and parked to see a man emerge from his house and drive away in the opposite direction. She saw his knuckles turn white from the grip he had on the steering wheel. Caruso pulled his truck into the drive and rested his head on the steering wheel as he contemplated his next move. His rage was still boiling when he entered the house. His wife called out from the bedroom. "Have you come back for seconds already?"

Tally could surmise his wife thought her lover had returned. When she saw Caruso instead, her hands flew to her mouth.

His first blow crushed her jaw before she could begin to explain what was going on. A second put her out cold. Caruso surveyed the room. Two wine glasses sat on the bedside table along with an ashtray with spent butts. He had never smoked, and neither had she. He stepped on something that must have made a sound. When he bent down to look, he found a condom wrapper and the used condom lying next to the bed. The man's total disregard for Caruso's home fueled his rage higher. Caruso walked into the bathroom and took his straight razor from the cabinet. He smiled as he drew the sharp edge across her throat, and blood began to run down onto the bed linens. When her heart stopped pumping, Caruso wrapped her lifeless body in the bedspread, then carried her to the back of his truck. The storm had arrived in earnest as he pulled out of his drive. He drove to a remote, wooded area and placed her body in a wooden shack. Caruso snapped the straight razor and tossed the sections in different watery areas on the way back to his home. Casper poured a gallon of bleach onto the bed of his truck, then used a high-powered nozzle to rinse any blood residue from his vehicle.

The next scene showed a dejected Caruso sitting on his front porch, the rain pouring down, soaking him to the bone as he watched blue lights appear in his driveway.

Tally listened to his perfect performance of a hard-working, offshore man who evacuated the platform with his crew, only to come home to find his wife missing and their bed full of blood. The forensics team had a plethora of DNA evidence from semen, saliva, and fingerprints, enough to quickly come up with a viable suspect. Even though there wasn't a body, the amount of blood soaked into the bed was enough to indicate the victim had bled out and couldn't have survived.

Caruso played the role of a grieving spouse in a perfect performance. During his testimony at the trial, he stared at Turner as he repeated his grisly tale of coming home to find his loving wife missing and their bed filled with blood. After the closing arguments, Caruso had to be physically restrained when the man was given a guilty sentence for the murder.

With a final clap of thunder, the vision was gone. Tally picked up her pen and started making notes.

†

The guard knocked on the door. "It's time for his lunch," he said.

Caruso stood up to be cuffed for transport. "Eat a good lunch. The last one is going to take you and your merry little band on a field trip." He smiled and picked up his Bible and then shuffled out the door.

†

Blair walked into the smaller room where Tally was still making notes.

"I guess you heard we have an adventure this afternoon. As soon as Tally finishes, let's head back for some more brisket." Blair smiled at Linda and Jamie. "You can't get too much of a good thing."

"You don't have to twist my arm." Jamie grinned. "I'm ordering more of those deviled eggs today."

"They were pretty good," Linda agreed.

Tally looked up from her notepad. "I need one of you to look something up for me before we go."

"Sure, what do you need?" Linda asked. She was still seated in front of her laptop.

Tally shocked them when she said, "The name of Caruso's wife."

"His wife?" Blair asked.

"Yes, I think it will play a role in our adventure today."

Jamie grabbed a stack of papers and looked at the original list Caruso had given them. There was no one with the last name of Caruso. "No Caruso here," he said, holding the list out to Blair.

They watched as Linda keyed up the search engine and began typing in her query. "Bingo. His wife was Caroline Murray Caruso and get this, she was murdered in two thousand and two. They never found the body, but the killer was found guilty and is serving a life sentence. Oh, snap. Right here in this same prison."

"There is a Caroline Murray," Jamie reported.

Tally looked at Blair. "He was innocent. Not completely, because he was sleeping with Caruso's wife while he was working offshore, but he didn't kill her."

"So, she was his first," Blair said. "Who does it say was the killer?"

Linda looked back at the file. "Gary Turner," she answered.

"Okay, after lunch, Tally and I will meet with the warden." She looked at Linda. "I want you to pull up everything you can find about the case. Jamie, I want you to follow up with the locals on the other victims if we haven't heard back from them." She shook her head. "He's saving his best for last, but is that all he has planned?"

"I wish I had that answer," Tally said. "Let's go. I'm starved."

†

The rain had stopped when they stepped outside. "Let me go get my car, and I'll pick you up." Jamie jogged across the parking lot, dodging puddles of muddy water.

Linda watched him with a growing smile. "You ride up front," Blair told her when Jamie pulled up.

Linda nodded and climbed into the passenger seat while Jamie opened doors for Blair and Tally.

†

"Damn, that rain just makes things steamier," Blair groaned when they walked out of the restaurant. "I guess I have to suck it up. We may be outside for a while today."

"Nothing like the humidity in the south," Jamie chuckled. "Hopefully, we won't be sent to an area with mosquitoes the size of small birds," he teased.

"You've got to remember to watch out for snakes, too, this time of year," Linda added in a serious tone.

"Well aren't you just a bundle of good news," Blair said. "Let's get this party started."

CHAPTER EIGHT

Tally and Blair were ushered into the warden's office. "What can I do for you, ladies?"

Blair settled into her seat. "Caruso is holding out his final victim reveal until this afternoon. He is expecting Ms. Rainwater and me to attend to this one personally."

The warden laughed. "Caruso's always had a set of balls on him."

"We also need to give you some information on another one of your inmates?" Blair replied.

"Who?" the warden asked.

Tally said, "Gary Turner. He's serving life here."

"I know Turner. He's been a model citizen here. What does he have to do with Caruso?"

Blair looked at him. "I believe we will uncover evidence today that will prove he was wrongly convicted."

The warden looked shocked. "You know we hate that term. What have you found out that you haven't told me yet? What does this have to do with Caruso?"

"Turner was convicted of killing Caruso's wife," Blair informed him.

"Good grief, and they've been housed here together. We totally screwed the pooch on that one. At least they are housed in two separate units."

"When we resume our interview this afternoon, I think we'll get on tape how Caruso framed Turner for the death of his wife. We have evidence which leads us to believe she was his first victim."

"Well, I'll be damned. Wouldn't that be a hoot? He'd free a wronged man just as he was about to be executed."

Blair nodded. "I just think it's another way for him to get a little more media coverage. I don't think he's forgiven Turner for screwing his wife and ruining his marriage. He's not had a huge change of heart about his own guilt. Still remorseless as ever."

The warden nodded. "How are his other leads panning out?"

"So far, he's been helpful. We will be able to close a couple of them even though he was never connected to them. For one, there was not a body, but he's provided enough information we can confirm his story. We are awaiting confirmation on a few others." Blair smiled. "I think this last one will be much more challenging, especially if it does turn out to be his wife."

"That is just chocked full of irony," the warden chuckled.

"If we can provide the evidence, will you set the system in motion to get the Turner case overturned?" Tally asked.

"Most definitely. We don't want to keep Turner in custody any longer than we already have. It may take some time, though. The wheels of justice can turn slowly, especially if it involves an erroneous conviction."

"I'm sure they had plenty of circumstantial evidence to gain a conviction," Blair replied. "I've seen convictions on much less."

"That is so true," the warden agreed.

"On a separate note, I mentioned I might provide Caruso a special meal if everything panned out. Would there be an issue if I had some chicken-fried steak sent to him?"

The warden chuckled. "Normally, it would be against the rules. Since Caruso has been cooperative in helping you close ten cases and possibly freeing an innocent man, I think an exception is in order."

"Thank you. I'll make the arrangements with Agent Enzo when we are through."

"It's the least I can do for your team's hard work. Let me know if there is anything else."

"Thank you." Blair and Tally stood to leave. "We may not return after today, so thank you for the hospitality and the tip on the brisket."

"Too danged good to not have you at least try it," he grinned.

Tally smiled broadly at him. "It was awesome. We may have it again before we leave."

†

They left the Warden's office and walked back to the conference room. Blair turned to Linda. "As soon as we finish here, I'd like you to send a copy of this next interview to the warden. It will be critical in appealing for Turner's release."

"I'll be on it like white on rice," Linda purred.

Blair chuckled at Linda's response.

Jamie ended a phone call. "We got confirmation on the last two victims. One more, and it's a wrap."

"Before I forget to say it, thanks for helping us out this week. You've both been a tremendous asset to Tally and me," Blair said.

"It has been an honor to work with the three of you," Jamie replied. "I've experienced more in the last few days than I did my first few months on the job."

Tally smiled at them. "Thank you. I hope you know if you ever need our assistance, you can contact us and we'll be there."

"It was a great pleasure working with you, but I hope we don't need you to come help anytime soon." Linda winked. "If only evil would take a vacation."

"Ain't that the truth." Blair chuckled. "I don't see us working ourselves out of a job anytime in the future."

"What are you expecting from this afternoon?" Jamie asked.

"I think he's going to have us locate this one instead of handing it off to the locals," Blair said. "We'll still need to contact the local jurisdiction once we know where we are headed." She turned to Tally. "I may need you to add some

135

information that you witnessed in your vision to ensure we get him to incriminate himself. That will be critical to getting Turner's conviction overturned."

"No problem," Tally replied. "I'm going to use the restroom, and I'll be right back."

Tally left the room and walked down the hall to the ladies room. As she was washing her hands, she looked at her image reflected in the mirror. Her eyes looked tired, and Tally was ready to be home back in their own bed. She loved her job assisting Blair, but they were both due for a break. Especially since their last trip had to be cut short. Hopefully, when they returned, they could get a week or two off.

"No time like the present," she said as she used a paper towel and tossed it in the garbage on her way out.

Caruso was just arriving at the conference room when she returned. "Welcome back." He grinned. "I hope you had a great lunch."

"We did. It was very delicious, thanks," Tally replied. She held the door and then followed Caruso and the guard into the room.

Jamie and Linda had gone. Tally turned on the video camera and also a small tape recorder as a backup device, then took her seat. She opened her notebook and waited for Blair to start the interview.

"I confirmed with the Warden that you could have a special meal delivered," Blair said after the guard left the room. "I'll have it delivered tomorrow if the rest of the information you give us pans out."

"I can taste that chicken-fried now," Caruso said, and licked his lips. "Extra gravy, too, please," he grinned.

"That shouldn't be a problem," Blair said. "You've done well so far, so we only have this one remaining. I sense this victim is special to you for some reason." Blair shuffled a stack of papers until she found the original list of victims. "I've checked off everyone except, a Caroline Murray."

Caruso relaxed back into his seat. He smiled at Blair. "Caroline Murray was her maiden name. I guess I should have added another name to the list. Gary Turner," he said.

Blair's brow shot up as she feigned surprise. "You killed a male? That's highly unlike you," she taunted.

Caruso glared at her. "I could have easily killed males, but females were much more fun. I didn't kill Turner, though, I did something much worse." Caruso chuckled.

"Were Turner and Caroline connected in some way?" Blair asked.

"Probably on more than one occasion," Caruso laughed. "I guess I'd better start at the beginning."

"I'm all ears," Blair answered.

"When I was a younger man, I worked offshore and made some terrific money. Don't get me wrong; it was long, hard hours working on an oil platform, and I was away from home and family for up to two weeks. It was simple when I was a single man." He gestured to Blair's list. "You can also add the last name, Caruso, to Caroline Murray's name. She was my wife."

"I didn't know you were married," Blair said. "I never remember you wearing a wedding band."

"I had one, but we never wore them for safety reasons while we were working on the rig. I left it on a small shelf beside the front door. It was the last thing I took off before I left to go back offshore, and the first thing I put on when I returned home. It was a simple gold band, but it meant the world to me."

Blair could hear his voice quiver slightly as he spoke.

"I met Caroline, a feisty red-haired beauty in my home town of Lufkin. She had moved to the area to attend Sam Houston and had grown to like the area, so she stayed after she graduated. She was a first-grade teacher. She loved kids, and we wanted to have several of her own."

"She sounds lovely," Blair said.

Caruso looked up at Blair, and she could see the moisture in his eyes. "She was a real looker, and I fell for her right away. We dated for three months and decided to marry." He paused. "We honeymooned in *Nawlins* and tried our best to return home pregnant. It didn't happen, though. It never did. After three years and a miscarriage, that dream was shattered."

"Did they ever find out why?" Blair asked with compassion.

"No, not completely, first it was scar tissue from some cysts on her ovaries, but they didn't think it was the total cause." Caruso paused a moment.

"Caroline was extremely depressed for a long time after the miscarriage, and it changed her. She wasn't the loving wife she used to be. I'd always look forward to coming home for the week and taking her out to a nice dinner, but then I would come home to find her in bed or deep into a bottle of wine." He shook the memory from his head. "I hated to see her like that, but nothing I tried would snap her out of the blues. Going to work every day and seeing all the kids only made it worse, so she quit her job as a teacher. We didn't need the money, but it had always been her passion."

138

"That's very sad. What happened after that?" Blair prompted.

"Another year passed and very little changed at home. We were evacuated from the oil rig one day due to a tropical storm headed our way, so I arrived home before she expected me. I was two days early, but she wasn't monitoring the weather, and I didn't call home, wanting to surprise her. But I was the one to get surprised."

Caruso paused to take a drink of water. This conversation was the longest he had shared since Blair and Tally had arrived.

"I arrived home at about ten that night, and as I was approaching the house, I saw a man race out and climb into a car and drive off. The rain was coming down in buckets. I didn't recognize the man nor the car, but my mind started whirling with rage. It didn't take a rocket scientist to figure out what was happening. I pulled into the driveway and sat for several minutes, trying to cool my rage. I had given Caroline everything I possibly could, except for a child. Her betrayal stung worse than the rain slapping me in the face as I raced to the door."

Caruso paused for several long seconds. "When I opened the door, the habit of putting my wedding band was forgotten. All I felt was rage and disappointment. When I started down the hallway, Caroline called out, 'Are you back for seconds, so soon,' thinking it was her lover returning. When she saw me in the doorway, she knew she had been caught. I don't know of any other way to describe it, but I snapped. Two hard blows to the woman I had adored left her bleeding and unconscious on the bed. I hadn't allowed her an opportunity to try to explain her infidelity."

139

He took another long drink. "My eyes surveyed the room. I saw an ashtray full of butts, two partially consumed glasses of wine, and a used condom and wrapper on the floor by the bed. Caroline never smoked."

Blair could see the rage burning in his eyes, even after all these years, as he talked about Caroline.

"My mind cleared enough to see the plan right before me to kill Caroline and frame her lover for the murder. There was so much forensic evidence left behind even the dumbest cops could put the pieces together and determine who the probable killer was. I just had to come up with the courage to do the deed."

"Is that where Gary Turner enters the picture?" Blair asked.

"Yeah, he was the poor sap balling my wife. He was the assistant principal at the school where she used to teach. I have no idea how long they had been screwing around, but it didn't matter. I had his balls in a vice, and I was going to make them both pay."

"Wow," Blair spoke.

"I went into the bathroom and opened the medicine cabinet. Caroline loved a smooth-skinned man, so I used a straight razor. For the first few years, she loved to shave me with it, but her interest in it waned after that." Caruso paused again to allow that memory to fade. "I opened the sharp razor and rushed back into the bedroom. Without hesitation, I raked the edge across her throat and watched as the blood and her life drained away. If I had paused, I probably couldn't have killed her."

Blair appeared to be making some notes while he took a short break. When she looked back up at him, she asked, "What happened next?"

"I didn't panic, which surprised me. I wrapped Caroline in the bedspread and carried her out and placed her in the back of my truck. It was still pouring down rain, and lightning bolts were flashing all around. I think the power may have gone out in the area as well. It was so dark, except for the brief flashes of lightning."

"Where did you take her?" Blair asked.

"My uncle had left me a small hunting cabin up close to a national park," he answered.

"Which park would that be?"

"Davy Crockett National Forest," he replied. "Some of the best hunting in Texas."

"Where did you leave her?" Blair prompted him to continue.

"There was a small outbuilding. I left Caroline in there until I could formalize the next part of my plan."

"Which was what?"

"To return home after thoroughly washing out the bed of my truck and play the part of the grief-stricken husband. Man, what a performance I gave. I was sitting on my front porch shivering in the cold rain, clutching my phone when the first blue lights arrived. I gave them my story and sat back to watch them do their work. It didn't take long for them to begin collecting the evidence and piece together what had happened. There was so much blood in the bed that no human could have lost that amount and still survived." He chuckled. "I allowed the paramedics to treat me for shock and then checked into a local hotel. I stayed there for weeks until the crime scene tape, and all the evidence, was removed. Then I put the house on the market. I couldn't live there with all those memories. That's when I moved close to Galveston and bought the boat."

"So, let me get this straight," Blair said, jotting more notes. "You killed her and framed Turner for her murder. Correct?"

"Yes. Turner had left so much evidence behind it made it easy. All school personnel had to have a thorough background screening, including fingerprints, so when they were entered, it didn't take long to produce a match. It was totally circumstantial since there was no body or remains, but it was enough for a jury to convict." Caruso laughed softly. "To make things even more ironic, the poor sonofabitch is housed two buildings down from me."

"No way," Blair said. "How could that happen?"

"I reckon it was some type of clerical mistake, but death row and lifers don't interact, ever, so I haven't seen him since he was sentenced. I hope he has suffered plenty for ruining my life. I imagine now they can let him go free."

"That is truly bizarre," Blair said. "Right here, in this very prison?"

"Yes, what a kick in the pants, huh?" Caruso laughed.

"So, then, I assume you didn't leave her in the outbuilding?" Blair asked.

"No, not for long. I waited until things calmed down a bit, and Turner was safely in custody. I drove back up from Galveston about a month later and buried her in the park. It had cooled down, and the stench of decomposition had faded enough to be tolerable. I put the bedspread holding her body in a trailer behind a four-wheeler and found a spot two miles from the camp to bury her. I knew the trail well from hunting over the years and knew the perfect spot."

"Did you map it out for us?" Blair asked.

Caruso grinned at her. "Only up to a certain point. Since this one is so dear to me, I wanted you and your team to recover her, not some bumbling local yokels. I left something with her I want you to retrieve for me."

"What could be left after all this time?" Blair asked, genuinely confused.

"My wedding band; I left it on Caroline's body, but in hindsight, I want to depart this world with the one object that genuinely brought me happiness. The day we were married was the greatest day of my life."

"How are we expected to find her if you haven't pinpointed the location for us?" Blair asked.

"When you reach the end of the map, you need to call me at the prison. I'm sure you can arrange that with the warden for your assistance in freeing an innocent man. I will ask you a question, one you can only answer if you're in the right place. If you answer correctly, I'll give you the exact spot to dig."

"That sounds easy enough," Blair said. "I'll make the arrangements, and we'll be on our way. I'll bring the ring back for you, but you know you won't get it until the day of your execution. Right?"

"That's all I need if for anyway. I trust that you will do the right thing and not try to play games with me," Caruso warned with a frown.

"You've trusted me up to this point," Blair reminded him. "Why would that change?"

"I can only have faith that you will do this last thing for me," Caruso said. He looked at the clock. "Time for me to go. Happy hunting. I'll be waiting for your call."

†

Blair and Tally left the room to speak with the others. "Pack up here and burn a DVD for the warden. I've got to see what we can do about getting a call through to Caruso, then we can roll."

†

The warden gave Blair permission to call on a private line to speak to Caruso.

"Agent Enzo will be bringing you a copy of the interview to use with Turner's appeal. I'm sure it will be enough, especially after we recover her remains."

"You'd better get rolling. That's going to be a bit of a ride. Be careful, and I hope to see you before you head back home."

"That's doubtful, but I do appreciate all your assistance," Blair stated and shook his hand.

Linda walked in and handed him a DVD of the interview.

Jamie had already packed the equipment and pulled his SUV around when they stepped outside. He opened the safe and took out three sidearms. "We better gear up," he said.

Blair took her weapon and placed it inside her shoulder rig.

144

"Key this address into your GPS, and let's get moving," Blair instructed Jamie. "What county is that located in?" she asked Linda.

"Lufkin is in Angelina County," Linda replied. "Since that was the scene of the crime, they would have jurisdiction."

"How far away are we?" Blair asked Jamie.

He looked at the GPS he was programming. "About, and hour and a half to this location."

"When we get within a half-hour, I want you to contact the local sheriff to meet us there. I don't want them out tromping around until we get closer."

Linda chuckled. "Understood. How much detail do you want me to give him?"

Blair smirked. "Just let him know we'll need his assistance, his coroner's assistance, and crime scene techs to recover the remains of a murder victim. Give him a name if you need it to convince him."

"I'll look up the information and have it ready," Linda replied.

Blair looked over at Tally who had pulled her sunglasses on. "You okay?"

Tally nodded. "I'm ready to go home."

"Soon," Blair promised.

"Not soon enough for me." Tally smiled.

†

The Texas landscape passed by the window in a blur as Jamie drove. Blair was lost in her thoughts, reviewing her conversation with Caruso, and hadn't noted the passage of time.

"We are close enough to call," Jamie said to Linda, breaking the silence.

"I'm on it," Linda replied.

Blair glanced at Tally, who had rested her head against the window and fallen asleep. She touched Tally's arm and gently shook her awake. "Hey, Sleeping Beauty. It's time to wake up."

Tally stretched. "I guess I nodded off, huh?"

"That's okay, it's been a fairly boring ride," Blair said. "We saw two bigfoots and the Loch Ness Monster while you were out."

"Bigfoots, I might believe, but Nessy? No way." Tally chuckled.

"Damn, I just thought of something. Is this vehicle four-wheel drive?" Blair asked Jamie.

"Shift on the fly." He grinned in the rearview mirror. "I've not taken this baby mud bogging, but I think she can take us where we need to go."

"I hope so. I'm not interested in getting stuck in a bog." Blair laughed. "Do you really go mud bogging?"

"Absolutely, ma'am. It's like a national pastime here in the South," he said with his most pronounced southern drawl. "The muddier your truck gets, the better."

"The sheriff should arrive just about the same time we do," Linda said. "Unless he knows a short cut."

†

The afternoon was quickly fading when they arrived at the hunt camp in Caruso's map. The sheriff had arrived, and when they stepped out of the SUV, Blair saw a coroner's van and crime scene vehicles approaching.

Blair introduced them once the locals had arrived and gave them a brief summary of the case.

"I'll be damned," the sheriff said. "He was smart enough to frame a not-so-innocent man. I bet he never sleeps with another man's wife again."

Blair turned to the coroner. "Do you want to hang back or join our merry little band?"

"I'd never pass on a chance to go on a hunt. I just hope this one is a success and not a wild goose chase."

"Let's do this then. We have the location programmed in, so y'all follow us," Jamie said.

CHAPTER NINE

Bobby Joiner stretched out in the deer stand. He had checked and double-checked his equipment three times in the last hour. Bobby confirmed the date and time on his watch. He was sure this was the right day. Since first reading an article about him three years ago, the nineteen-year-old had been a fan of Casper Caruso. He began corresponding with him, and they had developed their own system of code to communicate. For months, they had plotted Casper's revenge on the dyke FBI agent that had put him on death row. Casper trusted him to be the man for the job, and he would not let his mentor down. For weeks he had practiced the routine and made repairs to the tree stand. It gave him the perfect vantage point for a kill shot, just as Casper had planned. He was a genius and knew exactly how to lure her out into the open. Bobby wiped the sweat from his brow and took a big drink of water. *It wouldn't be long now*, he thought as the afternoon began to fade. The coming darkness would aid his escape as he could disappear into the forest and flee on the four-wheeled all-terrain vehicle he had concealed a quarter of a mile away. *Tick tock, your time is almost up, bitch.*

†

Tally watched their progress from the window. The Spanish moss hanging from the oak trees looked eerie, as they crawled down the rough trail. "I bet this place is scary at night," she whispered to Blair.

"I hope we'll be out before night comes," Blair answered.

"Halfway there," Jamie announced as he dodged another deep rut.

"Great, my teeth are already rattling," Linda teased. "Do you think you could avoid one of those major ruts?"

"You can drive on the way out," Jamie shot back at her.

Blair studied the hand-drawn map Caruso had given her. She prayed his memory was just as sharp as his other routes had been.

†

Bobby had pulled the letter from Casper out of his pocket to review his instructions. He knew precisely when to take the shot, and he understood his moment of glory was rapidly approaching.

"Just like clockwork," he said. Bobby folded the well-worn letter and tucked it safely into the pocket of his camouflage pants. He swatted a mosquito and watched a red-tailed hawk, floating through the sky as it hunted. "A good day to hunt," he said. The bird let out a long cry and plummeted toward the ground.

When Bobby heard the approach of several vehicles, he stood and took up his position. He felt his heart racing as he watched several people exit vehicles through his high-powered scope.

"Calm down, control your breathing," he spoke to himself. "You've practiced this a hundred times."

†

"You have arrived at your destination on the left," the voice from the GPS announced.

"Here we are," Jamie said and turned off the engine.

"There should be a large oak with a deer stand built in the crotch of the tree about two hundred yards, that way." Blair pointed to the left.

They waited for the rest of the vehicles to pull to a stop. The sheriff instructed his two deputies to bring shovels.

"I'm glad they thought to bring those," Jamie noted.

"Me, too," Linda said.

Blair walked at the front of the group with Tally right beside her. She spotted a massive oak, with boards that appeared to be the remains of a wooden deer stand dangling from the branches. "This has got to be it."

Tally shivered at the sight of the boards swaying in the light breeze. They gave her the feel of teeth grinding back and forth. Blair saw her shiver.

"Are you okay?"

"Yeah, this place just gives me the creeps," Tally replied, and crossed her arms, hugging her body tightly.

Blair pulled out her cell phone and prayed she would have service. She breathed a sigh of relief and pressed send on the number she had programmed into her phone. She heard a gruff sounding voice in the background, and then Caruso answered.

"You made good time, Agent Cooper."

"You missed your calling. You should have created maps," Blair told him. "I'm at the tree, but the deer stand has seen better days. Not much of it left."

"It was a great spot for hunting," Caruso replied. "I won't hold you up. It will be getting dark soon," he chuckled. "Walk around the back of the tree and tell me what you see carved in the bark."

Blair stepped over roots to walk to the rear of the tree. Carved deep into the oak were two sets of initials. *CC loves CM.* "Your initials and Caroline's initials," Blair spoke into the phone.

Caruso chuckled. "You are definitely at the right spot. Go back to the front of the tree and look straight ahead."

Blair returned to her original spot. "Okay. I'm there."

"Do you see twin oaks, about fifty yards ahead?" he asked.

"Twin oaks," she said. "Yes, I see them."

"Dig in the middle between them about three feet down, and you will find her. Don't forget to bring my ring. It should be near her right hand. See you soon, Agent Cooper." Caruso began laughing.

Blair was confused by his laughter, but took a step forward and tripped over a tree root.

A shot rang out, and Blair's body twisted and then fell to the ground.

†

Jamie pushed Tally to the ground beside Blair as he drew his weapon and squatted down. "Ambush," he cried out, as a second shot sailed over his head and bit into the tree.

"There!" The sheriff pointed to an area across an open field. A deer stand was high up in the tree, and they could see a shooter scrambling quickly down the tree.

Linda reached up to wipe blood from Jamie's jaw. A splinter of tree bark had flown into him to cause a small cut.

"You're bleeding."

"It's just a scratch," he said and smiled at her. "Stay with them." Then he sprinted towards the shooter, followed by the two deputies.

†

Tally shook her head. She struck the ground hard and was momentarily disoriented. Tally could hear laughter and looked to find it coming from Blair's cell phone. "You bastard," she screamed and scrambled over to Blair.

Linda had already reached Blair and saw the blood soaking into the white blouse beneath her blazer. "I need some scissors," she yelled back to the forensic crew who were still crouched low to the ground. "Now," she growled.

The coroner rushed over to help, as Blair opened her eyes.

She remembered a sharp sting to her left shoulder, then her body hitting the ground.

"Sonofabitch, what hit me?" she groaned.

"You've been shot," Tally said. "That bastard set up an ambush for us."

Linda used the section of Blair's blazer that had been cut away to apply pressure to the wound in her shoulder. "Just try to relax. Thankfully we have a doctor with us."

"Do I need to remind you that my patients have already expired by the time I get them," he announced, and then cringed at the glare he received from Linda.

"I don't give a fuck if they are dead. You're still a medical professional, and I'm counting on your skills to keep her from becoming one of your patients," she snapped at the middle-aged man.

Tally was holding Blair's hand. "Hang in there, honey. You're going to be fine." Tally was sure her voice was bereft of any confidence, but she had no other words of comfort that would come to her.

"Lift that up and let me take a look at it," the coroner said.

Linda lifted the soaked blazer while he examined the wound.

"She's lucky, the bullet went straight through and didn't hit any major arteries or bone," he reported.

One of the forensic guys rushed over carrying a first aid bag. "Let me help. I was a medic in the Marines. I saw plenty of these in Iraq." He smiled at Tally. "I'm Jack, and I promise to take good care of her."

"Thanks, Jack," Tally replied.

A shot rang out in the distance, and they looked in the direction the others had run.

†

"Fuck," Bobby growled as his shot hit her in the shoulder. It was supposed to be a perfect heart shot, but he saw her trip just as he squeezed the trigger, too late to stop the action. Bobby ejected the cartridge, aimed, and fired again. This time in his haste, he aimed high and hit the tree behind the group. More importantly, the second shot had indicated his location, and soon the pursuit would begin. He could hear startled male voices, and agents began rushing in his direction. The crush of the brush as they raced toward him echoed across the field. His time to go was now. There was no opportunity for another shot. He gathered his backpack and started quickly down the tree. He stumbled and twisted his ankle as he descended the tree, and when he touched the solid ground, he winced in pain. *I've got to run.* Bobby stopped long enough to fire one more shot in hopes of slowing down the pursuit. He gritted his teeth against the pain and rushed down his exit path.

†

Jamie heard the shot and stopped long enough to check the men in pursuit. No one had been hit, so he rushed ahead after the shooter. Jamie could see movement several hundred

154

yards ahead as his prey fled. He was dressed in camouflage, but the noise he made as he ran made him easy to track. Jamie noticed the shooter was running with an awkward gait. He wondered if he had injured himself exiting the deer stand.

†

Jack applied a pressure bandage and helped Blair to a sitting position.

"Let me up," Blair growled.

"No, ma'am, you stay right where you are for a few minutes," Jack said softly to her. His partner rushed to the coroner's van to retrieve a gurney.

Blair heard the metal clanking as he pushed it across the uneven ground. "There's no way in hell I'm getting on that thing."

"Okay, okay," Jack conceded. "We will need it for the remains, anyhow. Will you at least allow yourself to be carried? You're in no shape to walk right now."

"Please, Blair," Tally implored.

Blair's facial expression softened when she heard Tally's voice and turned to look at her.

"Please?" Tally repeated.

"Okay, I will. But no gurney from a death wagon."

"Gotcha," Jack said. He nodded to his partner, and they gently lifted her and carried her to the SUV. They placed her in the back seat. "Anyone have water or something to drink?" Jack asked as he wrapped a light blanket around her.

"I've got a cooler full of Gatorade," the coroner replied. "Hang on a sec."

When he returned moments later, Jack twisted off the top and assisted Blair in taking a drink. "We need to get you to a hospital," he told Blair and looked at Linda. "Her wound is not life threatening, but she needs to go soon. She lost a good bit of blood, and the longer she goes untreated, the higher the chance for complications."

Linda looked across the field to where Jamie and the others had disappeared and then back to Blair.

"You stay and help if you can. Tally and Jack can get me to the hospital," Blair said. "Is that a fact, Jack?" she teased.

"Yes, ma'am, it is." He grinned at her joke. He looked at his partner. "I'll be back as soon as I can hitch a ride back."

"You better bring reinforcements. This has got the makings for a long night."

"Gotcha," Jack said.

Tally climbed in beside Blair. "You call me and let me know what's going on," Blair said. "Oh, hell, where's my phone?"

"I've got it. Call me as soon as you know anything?" Tally said.

Linda looked at Blair. "You, too. We'll wrap up here and get to the hospital as soon as we can."

"Stay safe," Blair said. Her words were starting to slur a bit.

"Go," Linda told Jack, and closed the door.

†

Even injured, his unfamiliarity with the terrain made it difficult to catch up with the perp. Finally, after what seemed like an eternity, Jamie could see him as he crossed into a clearing. With energy, he wasn't sure he had, Jamie closed the distance and commanded the perp to halt. The young man limped on a few more steps and then turned to face him. Jamie had the man in his sights. The next move depended on the perp. Jamie's heart pounded in his chest as he waited for the man to react. He studied his face and saw the terror in the young man's eyes. *Damn, he's young, probably not even out of his teens.* The age of the shooter disappeared when Jamie saw him reaching for a gun.

†

Fuck, I'm not going to make it. Bobby could see his four-wheeler location barely a hundred yards ahead, but the cops were right behind him. Even if he could make it, he'd be shot before he could uncover his vehicle and escape. *It's decision time, Bobby, boy. Suicide by cop or prison time? There's no way you can survive being put in a cage, so I guess the decision just became easier. On my terms, or the cops,* he debated in a split second. *Mine.* He pulled out a pistol. He heard the young FBI Agent call out to him to drop his weapon. Bobby smiled, put the gun to his temple, and pulled the trigger.

†

Jamie watched in horror as the young man lifted the gun to his head. He would leave this world on his terms, not anyone else's. Before Jamie could plead with him to stop and think about his decision, the gunshot rang out. Jamie cringed as the front of the young man's head exploded.

157

The other officers arrived as the young man's lifeless body toppled to the ground.

"Shit," one of them said, then abruptly lost his lunch in the weeds.

"This crime scene just got a whole lot more complicated," the Sheriff said as he arrived. "What started out as a simple body recovery has turned into an attempted murder scene and now a suicide event. I will never complain about being bored again." He huffed, trying to catch his breath.

"Blair," Jamie cried out.

"You go. We ain't going anywhere soon. We'll secure this scene. Send the crime lab boys and coroner here first. This one is going to start smelling bad real soon."

"Got it," Jamie said and began jogging back across the field. The return trip didn't seem near as long as it had during the pursuit. He smiled when he saw Linda rushing toward him.

†

The SUV had barely gotten out of sight when a shot rang out in the distance. Linda looked at the coroner and crime scene tech. The coroner nodded his head.

"Go, there's nobody here that's going to do harm to us."

"Thanks," Linda said and started running toward the field.

The coroner turned to the tech. "I guess you better get on the phone and call for more help. We won't be home for supper. Hell, we might be lucky to make it for breakfast."

†

Jamie was surprised when Linda grabbed him in a hug and kissed him deeply. He took a step backward in shock.

"Don't you ever leave me behind again like that," she scolded him.

Jamie's shocked look softened as he took a step forward and took Linda in his arms. "I wouldn't have wanted you to see what just happened. I don't think I can ever unsee it."

Jamie looked down into her face, and Linda could see tears pooling in his eyes.

"How is Blair?"

"She's going to be okay. One of the crime scene techs was a medic and got her patched up. He and Tally have taken her to the hospital for treatment. What happened out there?" she nodded toward the sheriff and other men standing guard over the dead shooter.

"He must have injured himself coming out of the tree, but he still almost outran us. Another minute and he would have been on an ATV and on the road to escape. When I caught up to him, he knew his journey was over. He pulled out a pistol and took his life before I could try to talk him down." He sighed. "Not a pretty scene."

Linda reached out to caress his cheek. "Let's let the local boys handle that. We can work on recovering Caroline, or we can go to the hospital and sit in a waiting room."

Jamie smiled at her. "Let's stick to the assignment until we hear from Tally. Caroline deserves to be recovered."

As they walked back to the original scene, they could hear sirens wailing in the distance. "I think the cavalry is about to arrive."

159

Linda surprised him by taking his hand as they walked back to the crime scene. It felt good to have someone who cared for him. He kept her hand in his until they stepped into the mayhem.

†

"Do you still have those shovels?" Jamie asked the crime scene tech.

"Yeah, I do. Are you ready to start digging?" the tech answered.

"Let me update the coroner, and I'll be right over." He looked at Linda. "Will you start some measurements?"

"I'm on it." She pulled out her cell phone and began measuring the distance between the twin oaks while Jamie talked to the coroner.

"What happened out there?" the coroner asked.

"He chose suicide over time in prison. Not a pretty sight. The front half of his head is scattered about twenty feet."

The man sighed. "At least the cause of death will be simple to determine on this one. Not unlike what we will find in that grave."

"That one is easy too. The bastard slit her throat with a straight razor and then watched her bleed out."

"Is this Caruso? The Ghost of East Texas?" He chuckled. "I can't believe anyone would name a monster for anything other than what they are."

"Yep, one and the same," Jamie said. "I reckon I'd better get to digging."

"I've got another team on the way if you two need a ride to the hospital," he offered.

"We'll take you up on that when we hear from Ms. Rainwater," Jamie said.

"Rainwater? Is that the psychic that works with the FBI?" the coroner asked.

"Yes, it is. Ms. Rainwater is something else. Helped me clear a victim in Mississippi from fifteen years ago."

"No, shit. Another one of Caruso's?"

"Yeah, one of the early ones. Brutal bastard. Lethal injection is way too humane for him."

"I hear ya." He turned back to Jamie. "I'll help Agent Enzo set up some lights. I think it won't be long until we need them."

"Thanks," Jamie said and walked over to where Linda was measuring.

"Do you think you have the right spot?" he asked.

"Only one way to tell. Get to digging, big boy," she teased.

"The coroner is going to bring some lights over for y'all to set up. Darkness is falling fast."

Linda reached for his coat and shirt. "Nice," she teased when he was down to a muscle shirt.

Jamie felt himself blush and turned away to pick up a shovel. He looked at the tech. "Let's do this."

✝

Jack had called ahead to the hospital, and there was a trauma team awaiting them at the emergency room entrance. Jack and a nurse guided Blair onto a gurney, and she was rushed inside. "Let me go park this monster, and I'll bring you the keys and get an update while I'm waiting on my crew to pick me up." He saw an FBI jacket on the passenger seat. He picked it up and handed it to Tally. "Here you need to take this. It can feel like a meat locker in there sometimes."

Tally smiled and took the jacket. "Thanks for everything, Jack," Tally replied.

She walked into the emergency department and was ushered into an exam room.

"Agent Cooper has been taken for an x-ray, but she will return here in a few minutes," the nurse informed her. "Can I get you anything?"

"A margarita?" Tally teased.

"Sorry, fresh out. Water, coffee, or a soda?" she offered.

"Water will be fine. Thanks." Tally took a seat in the brightly lit room. When the nurse returned, she took the bottle. "Thanks again."

"I'll see you when our patient returns. I'm Mel, call me with that button if you need me," she said, pointing to a call button.

"Got it," Tally replied and took a long drink.

She listened to the loud ticking of the clock. "Damn, these places really should go digital." Tally knew she should probably report to the Director about Blair, but she knew he would turn around and contact Blair's dad. She would wait until Blair returned, and they were updated before getting Blair's permission to call. It would take Blair's voice to keep Thomas Cooper from jumping on the next jet to Texas.

Jack walked into the room and handed her the keys. "Any word yet?"

"They took her back for x-rays," Tally answered.

She heard Jack's radio sound. His team had arrived at the hospital. "Go, do what you need to do. Thanks for everything. Tell Jamie and Linda I'll call when I know something."

"I will." Jack smiled. "She's going to be okay. Sore as hell for a long time, but she'll recover completely."

Tally nodded as tears threatened to fall. Jack quietly left the room.

†

Ten minutes later, Tally returned from the restroom and heard Blair's angry voice coming from the room. "I don't need to spend any nights in the hospital. Just patch me up, and I'll be on my way."

"I don't recommend that," the ER physician warned her. "You need at least one night of observation."

"I agree with the good doctor," Tally said when she walked back into the room.

"Who are you?"

"Tally Rainwater, this cantankerous patient's partner. Also, someone who agrees with you, so back me up here."

"Hey," Blair said when she saw Tally. The pain medication they had given her was taking effect. She swayed slightly as she sat up on the exam table.

"One night is all he's asking," Tally said. "I'd be much more comfortable if you stayed the night."

Blair's frown softened. "Really? I promise you I'm okay."

"And you will be even better tomorrow," Tally replied. She turned back to the doctor. "What are we looking at?"

"A nasty exit wound that will take some time to heal, but she was fortunate the bullet only did soft tissue damage.

There is no shattered bone or ruptured artery to contend with. Someone was watching over her today."

"Amen to that. If you hadn't tripped on that root, I don't think we'd be here right now," Tally said. "I'm so glad your gracefulness left you for a second." She couldn't help but chuckle at the goofy expression on Blair's face.

"We've given her an injection for pain, and as soon as that takes effect, we will clean and dress the wound. I'd say we are about there," he said as Blair's eyes closed, and the grimace on her face disappeared.

"I'm going to step into the waiting room and make some calls. I will be back, though."

"Maybe we can have some room information for you by then."

"I'll be back in just a few." Tally walked out to the waiting room and found a quiet spot. "Who to call first? Linda will be easy. Let me start there."

Tally called Linda and gave them an update on Blair. Linda quickly informed her about the shooter committing suicide. Tally was glad to hear that they were still on site, attempting to recover Caroline's remains.

"There's not much you can do here besides wait. I'll call you with a room number as soon as she's officially admitted. Good luck with the search."

Now, Thomas or the Director? Tally decided on Thomas Cooper.

He took the news of Blair's injury much better than she anticipated. "I will be on a flight down first thing in the morning."

"I know you are as stubborn as Blair, so I'm going to let you two argue that out tomorrow. Yes, we're in Lufkin. I'll call you if anything changes. I'll tell her you love her when she wakes up. Love you, too, Dad."

The Director was next.

"Good Lord, have you called Thomas yet?" was his first question after Tally gave him Blair's status. She also gave him a quick update on the case and promised she'd have Blair call as soon as she could. She smiled when he said, "It sounds like you both did an excellent job. Thanks for keeping me up to date. Try to get some rest. You sound tired."

"I will. Thanks, Director." Tally ended the call and leaned her head against the wall. She was woken by a hand, gently shaking her.

"There you are," Mel said. "We're ready to move Agent Cooper to Room 215."

"That's great news." Tally stood and followed her back into the exam room.

Blair was resting soundly, so Tally sent a quick text to Linda. *Room 215.*

†

Jamie had worked up a sweat, but they were making progress. They had begun to uncover Caroline's remains. There was little of the bedspread remaining other than a few red fibers. He heard Linda's phone ping with a text and looked up. "More news on Blair?"

"A room number, Blair is in 215," Linda said.

"I bet that was a helluva battle to get her to stay," Jack said as he took the shovel from Jamie. "Let me spell you for a bit. Go get something to drink."

165

Jamie wiped his forehead with his arm. "I won't argue with that."

He stepped out of the small pit they had been digging and took a bottle of water from Linda. He turned back to Jack. "Keep an eye out for a man's gold wedding band."

Jack nodded and began digging.

†

Once Blair was settled in the private room, Tally entered and sat in a recliner next to the bed. The nurse came in to check her vitals.

"She's going to be out for a while. Why don't you grab something to eat, or can I have something sent from the cafeteria?"

"Thanks, I'm good for now. I may grab a sandwich later," Tally replied.

"Just let me know if you change your mind or you need anything. Caroline Caruso was a great person. She was my first-grade teacher and didn't deserve what happened to her."

Tally cocked her head in surprise. "I guess word travels fast around here."

"Jack filled me in when he found out you'd be admitted to our floor. We dated for a short time."

"Ah, Jack. He seems to be very nice," Tally replied.

"He is. Unfortunately, we didn't click as a couple, but he's a good friend. Don't laugh, but my name is Diane."

Tally stifled her laugh. "Jack and Diane. You're kidding me?"

"Probably why we didn't click. We were teased unmercifully by our friends. It's all good though, I met the

166

right one, and we're engaged." She held her hand up to show Tally the ring.

"Congratulations," Tally replied, and she heard Diane being paged to the nurse's station.

"I'll return later. Get some rest."

Tally watched the gentle rise and fall of Blair's breathing. The rhythmic beat of her heartbeat on the monitor relaxed Tally, and she felt her eyes growing heavy. She curled into a ball, and the last she remembered was Diane tucking a warm blanket around her body.

†

When Caroline's body was uncovered entirely, Jamie bent down and picked up a small round object. He dusted the dirt from it and saw that it was the wedding band Caruso had asked Blair to retrieve. Jamie slipped it into his pocket and stepped from the pit. He smiled at Linda.

"I think we can go now and let the locals finish up here."

The coroner was walking over to him. "You might want to take a photo of this. I can't give you the original, though." He held out a well-worn piece of paper. "Took it from the perp's pocket. His name was Bobby Joiner, and he appears to be a disciple of Caruso."

Linda took the paper, unfolded it, and snapped several photographs. Then she offered it to Jamie. He read the letter and then gave it back to the coroner.

"Seems like they've been planning this for a while."

"That would be my guess, too," he said as he dropped the letter into a plastic evidence bag. "I hope Agent Cooper recovers well. Please give her my regards," he said and walked to his vehicle.

Jack chuckled as he watched him drive away. Linda and Jamie turned to look at him.

"Come on, I'll give you a ride. I would have sent you with the coroner, but I think you want to arrive in one piece. He's dang near blind as a bat at night."

Jamie smiled. "Thanks. We've had enough excitement for one day."

Jack tossed a towel to Jamie. "You want to wipe down a bit? You worked up a sweat today."

"Yeah, I did." Jamie peeled off his sweaty T-shirt and used the towel to wipe down his chest and arms. Linda took it and wiped down his back, then handed him his dress shirt. She couldn't help but smile as she admired the ripped abs and broad shoulders.

She draped his blazer and tie over her arm. "I don't think you'll need either of these."

Jamie put his soaked shirt in a plastic crime scene bag. "That was definitely starting to become offensive." He grinned at Linda.

"We'll let you take the jump seat then," Jack winked to Linda. "That way, you'll stay downwind of us."

Jamie nodded. "That's probably a good idea."

"If you're ready, we can head to the hospital. Blair should be settled in her room and snoozing away by now." Jack grinned. "Tally has her hands full with that one."

"That she does," Jamie replied.

CHAPTER TEN

"Thanks for dropping us off, Jack," Jamie said when they reached the hospital.

"My pleasure. Blair's nurse is a good friend of mine, so if you need anything, just ask, and she can give me a call."

"Will do." He climbed out of the vehicle and opened the door for Linda.

Jamie dropped the bag with the sweaty shirt in the garbage at the front door. "I've got plenty of them." He smiled at Linda's grin. "No need to funk up the hospital."

Linda nodded. "I don't know about you, but I'm starving."

Jamie looked at his watch. "It's late, but maybe the snack bar is still open. I could eat, and I'd bet Tally hasn't eaten anything."

They followed the signs to locate the snack bar and found it didn't close for thirty minutes.

Jamie ordered three double bacon cheeseburgers and fries. "Grab some drinks from the cooler," he said to Linda.

"What if I wanted chicken?" Linda teased.

Jamie snapped his head around. "Do you want a chicken sandwich? I can still order one."

"No, I'm just giving you shit," she answered. "Who doesn't like bacon cheeseburgers?"

"It would be totally un-American," Jamie replied.

They carried the bags of food to the elevator and pushed the button to the second floor. A nurse was riding up with them.

"Man, those smell good," she said as the door closed behind them. "If it was just one of you, I'd consider a burger snatching," she joked.

"We'd be more than glad to share," Linda said as they walked onto the second floor.

"Thanks, are you looking for 215?"

"Yes, ma'am, how'd you guess?"

The nurse pointed to *FBI* on Linda's jacket. "It's not hard to assume you are here to see Agent Cooper. I'm Diane, her nurse for tonight."

"God bless you then. You deserve a hamburger for taking care of Blair. I'll run down and get another," Jamie offered.

"I was just kidding. I've got a wedding dress I have to fit into in three more months. Thanks for the offer, though.

Agent Cooper has been out since she arrived on the floor. The smell of those burgers might cause her to stir." She nodded down the hall. "Second room on the left. I'll be down to check on her in a few."

"Thanks, Diane," Linda replied and followed Jamie down the hall.

When they entered the room, Tally was sleeping soundly in the recliner, curled up in a ball. Surprisingly, Blair was awake, lying on her side, watching Tally sleep.

"Hey," Jamie whispered. "We didn't expect you to be awake. How are you feeling?"

"Like I've been hit by a Mack truck. Multiple times, but I think I'll live," Blair answered.

"Blair," Tally said as her eyes opened.

"I'm right here, sweetie." Blair reached out with her right hand to touch Tally. "Jamie and Linda are here."

Tally sat up in the chair. "I don't know what you have in that bag that smells delicious, but I'll fight whoever I need to for it."

"Jamie bought us bacon cheeseburgers and fries," Linda said.

Tally looked at Blair. "You feel like eating?"

"I could eat a little, but not one of those monster sandwiches he just pulled out," Blair teased.

"Split one with me then?" Tally suggested.

"I could probably handle that. Will that be enough for you?"

"Uh, huh. I'm not sure I can eat half." Tally looked at Jamie. "Did they put half a steer on there?"

"Everything's bigger in Texas," Linda reminded them.

"Damn, that's huge," Tally said.

Blair raised the head of her bed to a sitting position. "We can use the bed table for our dining room table," she instructed Jamie.

He walked over and rolled it to the side of the bed.

Diane knocked and walked into the room with two folding chairs. "Sorry, these are the only extras I could find."

"They will be perfect," Linda said.

"Hey, look who's awake," Diane said when she saw Blair sitting up. "I'm your nurse, Diane. How are you feeling?"

"Like I've been shot, and hungry," Blair answered. "Thanks for taking care of me."

"You've been a piece of cake so far, so let's don't change a thing. You're due for some pain medicine soon, but you can eat, and I'll bring it later. Just don't overeat."

"Yes, ma'am," Blair replied. "Oh, dear Lord, are those seasoned fries."

Diane chuckled and left the room.

"Do you want to hear a good one?" Tally asked. Blair nodded.

"Your nurse and Jack used to date."

Blair looked confused. "What?"

"Jack and Diane. John Cougar Mellencamp," Tally answered.

"Oh, I get it now." Blair chuckled. "Jack and Diane. That is a good one."

After eating, Blair started to fade. Tally pushed the call button and told Diane she'd better hurry if she planned to get a pain pill in Blair.

Jamie looked at Tally. "Do you plan to stay the night with Blair? I know that's probably a silly question."

"Yes, I do. The two of you don't need to stay, though. Go, get a good night's rest and come back tomorrow. Her dad's flying in, but I don't have details yet."

Blair was still awake enough to hear that. "Did you say Dad is coming?"

"Yes, darling. I had to call the Director, so I thought I'd save him the call and called your dad first. He's as stubborn as you and wouldn't hear anything about not coming down."

"Dang, Tally, you know how he is." Blair gave her a goofy grin.

"Uh, huh, I do. I live with Thomas' carbon copy, remember."

"Thomas Cooper is your father?" Jamie asked. "Damn, this just gets better and better."

Linda looked at him with a question. "The legendary profiler, Thomas Cooper," he replied.

"Oh, shit. Really?" Linda grinned. "Two FBI legends in one family."

"Ha! I'm far from a legend," Blair said.

"You're getting there quickly," Jamie said. "They call you the Queen of Serial Killers at the Academy."

Blair chuckled. "That's hilarious."

When she fell silent, Tally could tell the pain medications were kicking in. She looked at the clock. "It's after eleven. You two had better scoot. You still have over an hour to drive."

"Are you going to be okay here?" Jamie asked.

"Do you want us to bring a bag with some clean clothes for you two?" Linda asked.

"That would be great. I have a smaller bag, the one from our night in Baton Rouge," she said to Jamie. "You can pick

173

us out two pairs of shorts, shirts, tennis shoes, and our hygiene stuff. We can shower here and be ready to bolt as soon as she gets discharged." Tally handed Linda her room key. "Be prepared to tell us about the events after we left in the morning. Blair will want a blow-by-blow accounting."

"Yes, ma'am," Jamie said.

"Thanks for the fantastic burger. It really hit the spot," Tally said. "Oh, I guess you'll need these. You're parked out by the emergency department." She handed him the car keys.

"Alright, we'll be here in the morning. Let me know if we need to pick up Blair's dad from the airport or anything."

"Thanks, Jamie. I will. Y'all drive safe. Text me when you get back to the hotel, please."

"Yes, Mom," Jamie said. "Call if you need anything else."

"Oh, one other thing. Lock this up for Blair." She handed Blair's sidearm to Jamie.

"Will do. See you tomorrow."

"Goodnight," Tally said. Once they left, she reclined back and wrapped the blanket around her.

Diane opened the door and lowered the lights to keep from waking either of the occupants.

†

Tally's sleep was disrupted by dreams of Blair being shot. Instead of the shoulder wound, Blair had been shot through the heart. Tally bolted upright in the recliner, and her head whipped around to find Blair sleeping peacefully. Diane was standing at the end of the bed monitoring Blair's vitals.

"Are you okay?" she asked when Tally awakened so suddenly.

Tally nodded. "Just a bad dream. I dreamed the shot hit the intended target."

Diane smiled. "As you can see, Blair is resting well. She's a remarkably strong woman and will heal in no time. I'll be getting off shift in an hour, but I think she'll be discharged after the doc makes his rounds about ten this morning." She saw Tally smile. "I just brewed a fresh pot of coffee, if you'd like a cup."

Tally grinned. "Thanks. I don't think I'll be doing any more sleeping this morning."

"Cream and sugar?"

"Lots of both," Tally replied.

"I'll be right back then." Diane left the room.

Tally glanced at the clock and gave thanks that at least the hospital had placed digital ones in its patient rooms. The ticking of the clock in the emergency department had really worn on her nerves. She picked up her phone and saw a message from Thomas.

I'll be there by nine.

The message had come in over an hour ago, but Tally thought she'd still answer. *Do you need a ride from the airport?* There was no immediate answer, so she assumed he was still in flight.

Diane returned with her coffee and a handful of condiments. "If this isn't enough, let me know."

"Thanks. If I don't see you before you leave, we really appreciate all you did for Blair."

"Just doing my job, ma'am," Diane said with a wink. "I hope she recovers quickly and y'all stay safe. The world is full of monsters, as I'm sure you both are painfully aware."

"Yes, it is," Tally replied. "Best of luck with your wedding. I hope it will be a grand adventure for you both."

"Thanks. Have a safe trip home."

Tally prepared her coffee and snuggled back into the blanket. She sipped the strong brew as she watched Blair sleep. Motion out of the corner of her eye caught her attention, and she glanced at the television that she hadn't realized was on. The sound was muted, but the screen flashed video of a gurney carrying a body bag, and the ticker tape at the bottom revealed the remains of murder victim, Caroline Caruso, being recovered. A picture of a pretty, red-haired woman flashed on the screen and then a mug shot of Caruso with his ever-present smug expression. A view of a young man came across next. He was described as Bobby Joiner, a co-conspirator of Casper Caruso, who had attempted to murder FBI Agent Blair Cooper. The FBI press photo of Blair came up.

"Not my best side," Blair said and turned up the volume.

"Good morning, sweetie," Tally said.

With the volume turned up, they listened as the reporter gave an account of the night's events from an interview with the sheriff. "Agent Cooper is in fair condition at the local hospital," he stated.

"Good Lord, he should know by now you never release that kind of information," Blair groaned.

Chuckling, Tally stood and walked to the window. She peered through the blinds. "Yep, the vultures are circling."

She started to turn back to Blair and stopped. "Oh, no," she said.

Blair painfully sat up on the bed. "What's the matter?"

"Poor Jamie and Linda have just arrived, and the scavengers are rushing toward them." Tally watched as Jamie and Linda exited the vehicle, and Jamie pulled out the suitcase. They both kept their heads down and plowed through the small crowd of reporters and cameras. "They made it through safely." Tally chuckled.

"Aside from football season, yesterday was probably a big news day for them," Blair said.

Tally was still standing at the window when Diane came into the room. "I guess you see the crowd outside?"

"Yeah, the news coverage has got them all stirred up," Blair said.

"Don't worry. The hospital has a secure exit you can use when you are discharged."

"Thanks, Diane. There's nothing worse than a flock of prying reporters first thing in the morning," Blair teased.

A soft knock sounded on the door, and then it opened. Linda and Jamie entered with a small suitcase. Jamie grinned at Blair. "You've caused quite a ruckus in this little town. The parking lot is filling with reporters and TV crews."

"We heard," Blair said and pointed to the TV. "Caruso's last fifteen minutes of fame have begun."

Linda looked at Tally. "I hope what I picked out for y'all to wear is okay." She motioned toward the suitcase.

"Thank you so much, Linda." Tally looked at Diane. "Can she have a shower, if we promise not to wet the dressing?"

"Yes, but no water other than a toothbrush above her chest. Oh, and maybe just a bit to calm down that wild case of bedhead," Diane smirked. "There's a hand-held wand and a shower chair you should use. Tiffany will be your nurse this morning, so call if you need anything."

"Thanks, Diane," Blair said.

"You two sure are up early. Did you sleep at all?" Tally grinned. She noticed a blush on Jamie's neck.

"Yes, we wanted to return early if Blair was discharged first thing," Jamie quickly answered. He pulled out the two folding chairs for them to take a seat.

"Did you have breakfast?" Blair asked.

"We grabbed a coffee on the way," Linda reported.

"I am in dire need of a shower. Why don't you two go grab some breakfast while I get cleaned up?" Blair suggested.

"Yes, ma'am," Jamie stood and moved the chairs out of her path. "May we bring you anything? I know what hospital food is like," he scowled.

"A biscuit and sausage or ham or bacon would be fine," Blair answered. "A large fountain coke, too, please. For some reason, I'm craving that this morning."

"No problem. We'll see you in a half hour or so." He looked at Linda. "Let's grub."

†

They waited for the two agents to leave before Blair carefully climbed out of bed. "It's kind of breezy," she said as she held the backside of the hospital gown closed.

178

Tally laughed softly and opened the suitcase. "Go relieve your bladder, and I'll grab some hygiene supplies."

Blair walked into the bathroom. It did feel good to pee. She glanced at the shower and saw Diane had already positioned a shower chair in place. She dropped the gown into a bin and sat on the chair to await Tally.

"That was quick," Tally said when she entered the bathroom. She set the hygiene kit on the top of the toilet tank.

"When ya gotta go, you gotta go," Blair replied. "Do you want me to start the water?"

"Sure, just be careful of your wound."

When Blair was showered, dressed, and sitting back up in bed, Tally ran through a quick shower and dressed. When she placed her dirty clothes in the bag, she looked at Blair. "Do you need anything?"

"Yes, I do." She pointed to her lips.

Tally leaned over and kissed her lover.

"Ah, that's better."

Tally placed the plastic bag with Blair's shoes and pants in the suitcase and looked over at Blair. "Your blouse and blazer were toast, so we tossed them in the ER."

"No problem," Blair said as she leaned back in the bed.

"How are you feeling?"

"A bit on the weak side and my shoulder is aching, but not horribly."

"The weakness is probably from the blood loss. Could be why you're craving fluids, too. Do you want something for pain?"

"Yes, but nothing narcotic," Blair answered.

Tally used the call button for Tiffany to request something for pain.

Tiffany brought it a few moments later, and Thomas followed her into the room.

"You're early," Tally said as she hugged and kissed him.

"We caught a tailwind." He chuckled and turned to Blair. "How are you feeling?"

"A bit sore, but okay. You didn't have to come, Dad." Blair leaned forward to kiss him.

"I know, but I was getting bored at home. I also love the brisket down here." He chuckled.

"That's a long way to come for a meal," Blair teased him.

"Have you had it yet?" he asked.

"Yes, several times," Blair answered.

"Then you know it was worth the flight." He chuckled.

Tally sat on the bed next to Blair and gave Thomas the recliner. "Thanks for calling me, Tally. I know if it were up to Blair, I wouldn't have been called."

"I waited until she was sedated and snuck a call in." Tally winked. "She didn't know until later."

"It's good to see you, Dad. You're getting all nice and tanned. I guess retirement is treating you well." Blair reached for her dad's hand.

"It is, but there's only so much golf and fishing I can take. I needed a short road trip and, boom, you get shot. No pun intended."

180

"Of course not." Tally laughed at his joke.

The door opened, and Linda and Jamie returned with bags of food. "Are we interrupting?" Jamie asked.

"Get your butts in here with that coke," Blair ordered. "Dad, this is Jamie and Linda. Guys, here is your legend you've been dying to meet."

"Ha!" Thomas answered. "Hello, you two. Thanks for being here to help Tally and Blair."

"It's been our pleasure," Linda said as she reached in front of Tally to hand Blair her coke.

"Something told me to get extras," Jamie said. He pulled out bottles of coke and juice. Then four biscuits. "Ham, bacon, sausage, and country ham," he announced.

"I'll take the regular ham," Blair said.

"Thomas, what's your preference?" Tally asked.

He smiled at Tally. "I'll take that country ham if you don't mind. What are the youngsters going to eat?"

"We had a full breakfast while these two were getting cleaned up, sir," Jamie reported.

"Ah, okay, then. Hand me a biscuit and some of that apple juice."

Jamie served him and pulled out the chairs for him and Linda.

Blair swallowed a bite of biscuit and looked at Jamie. "Are you ready to tell us what happened after I went down?"

Jamie nodded. "The perp, a nineteen-year-old Bobby Joiner, was positioned in a tree stand across from where we were. He was a disciple of Caruso and had been corresponding with him for months, apparently to plan the ambush. Ironically, he was a criminology student at Sam Houston."

181

"How did you make a connection with Caruso?" Thomas asked.

"He had this in his pocket," Jamie replied and pulled up the scanned image of the letter from Caruso to Joiner on his phone. "It's coded, but the message is pretty clear."

Thomas read through the letter and handed the phone to Blair.

"It was a miracle you tripped when you did, or you would have taken a shot to your heart. Joiner tried to get off a second shot, but he aimed high, and it hit the tree behind us."

"Is that why you have a nick to your face?" Blair asked.

"Yeah, a scratch from a piece of flying bark," he said.

"It was more than a scratch," Linda added. "You were bleeding pretty good for a bit."

Jamie chuckled and pointed to his cheek. "You can see it's far from life-threatening."

Tally smiled at him. She really liked the two young agents.

"Anyhow, the second shot gave us an idea of his location, and we started our pursuit. He must have injured himself coming down from the tree. He was limping as he fled. We caught up with him about a hundred yards short of the four-wheeler he had concealed for a getaway vehicle."

Jamie took a sip of his drink. Tally could sense the next part was difficult for Jamie.

"When I had him in my sights, he turned and knew there was no escape. Joiner decided to take his life rather than spend time in prison. He lifted a pistol and took his life before I could stop him."

Blair smiled. "I know it's hard to witness that, but we can be thankful he didn't choose suicide by cop. It's never easy to shoot anyone."

"I don't think I'll forget that for a long time," Jamie said. He cleared his throat. "After that, I returned to assist Jack and the crime scene techs in recovering Caroline's body." He stood and placed his hand in his jeans pocket and pulled something out. He handed Blair the gold wedding band.

"You found it? Great job!" Blair smiled up at him.

Thomas cocked his head. "What's that?"

"Caruso used this, his wedding band, as a ruse to get us out to the ambush site. He wanted it recovered before he is executed in December. Caruso had revealed ten victims' locations, so I judged it was something we should do. I had no clue what he had planned."

"Are you going to give it to him?" Tally asked.

Blair looked at her lover. "I don't know yet. In a way, I feel I'd be admitting defeat if I gave it to him."

"I will support whatever decision you make," Tally told her.

"Caroline's remains were recovered so her family can give her a proper burial, and Turner can be freed from prison," Jamie said.

"Turner?" Thomas asked.

Blair nodded. "Caroline was Caruso's wife. He returned home from working on an oil platform to find she had been having an affair. He murdered her and then framed her lover, Turner, for the murder. Ironically, he is serving a life sentence at the same prison."

Thomas shook his head. "The same prison? Someone dropped the ball on that one."

"We've collected enough evidence to have his conviction overturned. The recovery of Caroline's remains was the last piece," Tally added.

†

The door swung slowly open, and a female doctor walked in. "No one told me I was missing a party," she said. "I'm Dr. Nelson. If I can clear the room for a few minutes, I'll take a look at your wound and get you out of here. Unless you want to stay?"

Blair sat up taller. "Go, go." She waved her hand to shoo her friends and dad from the room. "Not you, Tally. I need you to hear how to care for the wound."

"I won't keep her any longer than necessary," Dr. Nelson said as the room cleared, and Tiffany brought out a treatment tray. "I see you have a fan club waiting out front. Is there anyone who won't be recognized that we can have meet you at a secure exit?"

"Yes, I don't think they recognized my dad. At least he didn't mention it," Blair answered.

"Good, we can use your FBI team as a diversion, and we can get you away without troubles."

"Thanks, Doc," Blair said and then winced as she pulled the dressing off to examine the wound.

"Sorry, I know it's pretty tender. The wound looks clean, and there is minimal drainage." Dr. Nelson looked at Tally. "No offense, Tally, but I'd rather see Blair under the care of a wound specialist for a few weeks to treat this. Too much can go wrong if it doesn't heal properly."

"No offense, at all. We can make that happen." Tally replied.

"The dressing I'll put on here will be good for several days until I assume you can head home."

"Yes, we'll probably head out in a day or so," Blair replied.

"Don't hesitate to return here or any emergency department if things start to change. Fever, increased pain, bleeding, or heavy drainage." Dr. Nelson secured the new dressing. "I'm prescribing some antibiotics and something for pain. I noticed you didn't want a narcotic earlier. Do you have a sensitivity to them?"

"No, I just prefer to not use them unless absolutely necessary," Blair replied.

"No problem. I'll have your paperwork ready in just a few minutes. Maybe your diversion team can take the prescriptions and get them filled while they wait for you."

"That's a great idea, Doc," Blair smiled.

When she left the room, Jamie, Linda, and Thomas returned.

"Okay, so here's the escape plan." Blair looked at Linda and Jamie. "Will you take the suitcase and the prescriptions and head out as a diversion? Dad, I'm hoping you rented a car."

"I did," he replied. "A small SUV."

"Good. You are going to be our getaway driver. Tiffany will give you directions to a secure exit, and you can go out after Jamie and Linda. The media has already recognized them and hopefully will concentrate on them."

She turned to Jamie. "Get the prescriptions filled for me, please, and meet us at the hotel."

Tally handed him a fifty-dollar bill. "That should cover the medications."

"We will meet you back at the hotel as soon as we can. Dad has already said he wants brisket if y'all aren't sick of it already."

"Sounds wonderful," Jamie said. "Maybe more chicken-fried tonight?" he suggested.

"I love the way this young man thinks," Thomas said, and smiled.

Tally helped Blair into her tennis shoes as they waited.

When Tiffany brought in her discharge packet, the team jumped to action. Tiffany loaded Blair into a wheelchair and said, "Let's get you out of here."

†

Jamie and Linda rushed through the growing crowd to the SUV and climbed inside as Thomas walked unnoticed from the hospital. Jamie pulled up to the front entrance and parked as if waiting for someone to come outside. Jamie and Linda got a good laugh when they saw Thomas climb into his car and drive away. Then the door opened, and a nurse brought a woman out in a wheelchair. The crew flocked to her, and Jamie calmly put the SUV in gear and drove away.

†

Thomas drove his vehicle to the designated spot and watched as Blair, Tally, and Tiffany emerged from the hospital. "Thanks again for everything," Blair said from the front seat.

"Our pleasure, just don't show up again, unless it's to visit," Tiffany teased. "Make sure she keeps that arm in a sling for two weeks," she encouraged Tally. She looked at Thomas. "Drive safe."

Tiffany closed the door, and Thomas pulled away.

"Where to?" he asked Tally.

"I'm pulling up the directions now," Tally replied.

†

After another fantastic meal, they returned to the hotel and got Thomas a room. Blair was starting to fade and looked at them.

"If you don't mind, I think I'll lay down for a bit."

"Not at all, honey," Thomas said. "I think I'd like to continue my conversation with these two," he said, nodding to Linda and Jamie.

"We'd love that," Jamie answered. "Do you want to come to my room? I'm right across from Blair and Tally."

"That would be great. Let me stop off in my room to powder my nose, and I'll be right over." Thomas looked at Blair. "Get some rest. We can catch up over dinner."

†

Blair took her arm from the sling, then stretched out on the bed. Tally climbed in beside her.

"Are you feeling okay?"

"Yes, just sleepy. Linda and Jamie's excitement over meeting Dad was wearing me out." Blair laughed.

187

"I'm sure they will drill him with questions for a few hours," Tally said.

Blair grinned. "He'll eat it up. He loves to talk to young agents about his experiences. I can't believe he hasn't taken an instructor's role at the academy yet."

"Do you need another pillow?" Tally asked.

"Nope, I just need you beside me." Blair smiled. "I love you."

"Love you, too. What time should we plan on for dinner?"

"Six will be fine. That gives me a couple of hours to nap. You can go join the others if you want after I fall asleep. I know you enjoy Dad's stories too."

"I will," Tally said and leaned over to kiss Blair. "Get some sleep."

CHAPTER ELEVEN

When they returned to the hotel after dinner, they said goodbye to Linda. Blair, Tally, and Thomas would be flying out early the next morning.

"Dad's going to give us a lift to the airport, so why don't you sleep in a bit tomorrow," Blair told Jamie. "Are you heading home?"

"After lunch with Linda," he grinned.

"Fantastic," Tally smiled back to him. "I hope things work out with you two."

"Only time will tell," he said. "Thanks for teaching us so much this week. I hope you'll have a safe trip back."

"We will. Keep in touch," Tally said, and then hugged him goodbye.

†

When they landed at the airport, Thomas turned to them. "Do you need a ride home?"

"Thanks, but we left our car here, Dad," Blair replied. "If you're not too busy, why don't you come over later this week, and we'll grill some steaks?"

"That sounds great. I'll call, and we can set a night."

They separated at the baggage claim.

"Do you want me to go get the car?" Tally asked.

"If you don't mind. I'll get a porter for our bags and meet you out front."

"Good deal," Tally said. "I'll be around shortly."

†

"Just leave the bags for now," Blair said when they arrived home. "Let's go relax, and we can get them out later."

"Okay, sweetie, I'll just grab our small bags if you get the door."

Blair opened the door, and Tally took the bags with their laptops inside.

"Home, sweet home," Blair said once they were both inside. "I got a text from the Director while I was waiting for you. I'm on medical leave for the next month. I need to see a wound specialist, and after I'm cleared, I'd like to go someplace."

"Anywhere you want to go?" Tally asked.

"Maine," she grinned.

"That sounds like fun. We can do some research and make some plans this week." Blair looked tired from the early flight. "Nap time?"

"Yeah, do you mind?"

"Not at all. I'll bring in our bags and get laundry started. Anything in particular you want for dinner?"

Blair grinned. "Brisket."

Tally chuckled. "I guess one of us is going to have to learn how to cook it."

"Don't let me sleep more than three hours," Blair said.

"No problem. Get some rest. Love you."

"Love you too."

†

Tally unloaded the bags and began working on the laundry they had accumulated from their beach trip and Texas assignment. As she was sorting clothes, she felt something in Blair's pocket and reached in to pull out the gold wedding band Jamie had given her. Blair had yet to say what she was going to do with it, but she was steadfast in her denial of the special meal she had promised Caruso. Tally didn't blame her one bit. After all, the bastard tried to have her killed, and if it weren't for some luck, he would have succeeded.

Tally placed the ring in Blair's desk drawer and went about her laundry. She was almost certain Blair would fly to Texas to watch the execution. She would go to Texas with her, but she had no desire to witness the deed.

†

191

Blair's appointment with wound care went well, and the specialist told her she'd need one more dressing change in a week. After that, Tally could start doing daily dressings.

They were excited to plan a trip to Maine and printed several maps of areas they wanted to visit in the area.

Thomas came over on Friday, bearing three of the most massive steaks Tally had ever seen. He cooked them to perfection, and they enjoyed the evening spent with him on their deck.

†

When they left for their trip to Maine, Blair no longer had to wear a sling, which was terrific, but the cooler weather made her injury ache. They spent days walking along the beaches on the Maine Coast and visiting many local attractions. Their nights were filled with lovemaking and romantic candlelit dinners. Tally loved the relaxed look on Blair's face as they enjoyed exploring the shallow tide pools. She wished the stress-free days would last forever, but she knew that eventually reality would once more come crashing down around them, so she cherished every moment with Blair.

†

One night after a fabulous lobster dinner, they decided on a moonlit walk on the beach. The sea breeze had a chill to it, but it was a beautiful night. They walked farther and began to see flashing lights and heard sirens wailing along the shoreline road.

"I wonder what's going on?" Tally asked.

"I've no idea, but it looks like they are stopping just ahead of us. Let's go see if we can be of assistance," Blair suggested.

As they approached, they began passing searchers with flashlights scouring the beach. When Blair recognized them as law enforcement, they approached a young officer. "What's going on?" she asked.

The woman looked up and brushed the hair back from her face. The wind had picked up and was beginning to whip Tally's dark hair. "A young boy is missing. He's twelve and has been missing for hours. He left on his bicycle to do some beachcombing and has failed to return home. His frantic parents called us about twenty minutes ago. Have you seen him or any evidence of him on your way here?"

"No, we haven't seen a child and didn't have a clue to look for one," Blair said. "We are with the FBI and would like to help with the search."

The officer pointed toward the flashing lights. "You'll find Sheriff Boone and the parents up there."

"Thanks," Blair said as the woman walked on. She turned to Tally. "What do you think? I know we're on vacation, but maybe we, or you can help."

"It's worth a shot. Let's go," Tally answered.

†

When they arrived at a parking area, Blair asked for Sheriff Boone. A tall, lanky officer pointed them to a woman. "She's the Sheriff," he replied.

"Thanks," Blair answered, and they approached a small group. The sheriff was instructing a group of volunteers, and the child's parents were looking on with worried faces.

The sheriff looked up and frowned. "May I help you?" she asked a bit sharply.

"We are with the FBI, and we'd like to offer our assistance. I'm Special Agent Blair Cooper, and my partner is Tally Rainwater, a consultant for the Bureau." Blair handed the sheriff her identification."

The Sheriff cocked her head. Blair smiled. "We're on vacation."

"Thanks. We'd welcome any help you can offer." She looked at the boy's parents. "These are Jody's parents, June and Brian Colten."

June's voice quivered as she stepped forward. "Jody left to come down to do some beachcombing. He's been doing it for months, but he's usually home by dark. We've tried calling his cell phone, but it goes directly to voicemail." She broke into tears, and Brian slipped an arm around her shoulders to comfort his wife.

"How did Jody get here?" Tally asked.

"He rides his bike everywhere," Brian answered. "We found his bike parked over there," he added, and pointed to a bike locked to a railing.

"Do you have a picture of Jody?"

"Yes, we've already printed some out," the Sheriff replied and handed one to Blair.

Blair looked at Tally. Tally nodded. "I'd like to try," she told Blair.

Blair looked at the grieving parents and Sheriff Boone. "I'd like to offer a suggestion. Tally is a psychic that has worked with the FBI and me for several years. She's been extremely accurate in locating missing people."

"I thought you looked familiar," Sheriff Boone said. "Weren't you recently on the news for a case in Texas? Weren't you shot?" she asked, raising an eyebrow.

"I was, but I'm healing well," Blair smiled.

"Would you be okay with Tally touching Jody's bike to see if she can connect with him?"

Brian looked at June and then the Sheriff. "Right now, we'll do anything we can to find our son."

"Thanks," Tally said and walked away from the group to where the bike was parked. She smiled at the lock that encircled a wooden rail on a barrier fence. It was evident to her that he loved this bike. She took a final look at his picture and knelt down beside the bicycle. She placed her hand on the seat and closed her eyes. She opened her mind and sent out a plea for Lisa to appear. Tally was relieved when she saw movement in the darkness, and Lisa stepped forward.

"Hey, Tally, what's going on?"

"I need your help to find a lost boy. His name is Jody, and he's been missing for hours." She opened her eyes, so Lisa could see the picture of Jody.

"He's a cutie," Lisa replied.

"He comes down to search the beach for shells and other treasures. Jody's parents say he usually comes home before dark, but not tonight. They've tried calling, but his phone goes straight to voicemail."

"Come with me," Lisa said, and Tally felt herself drifting down the beach. The scene was earlier in the day, late afternoon as she could see a trail of footprints in the wet sand. They led to a small tidal pool where Jody had stopped to look at the fish and other creatures trapped in the shallows. The trail zigzagged down the beach, stopping at different pools for over a mile."

"Can you sense he's alive?" she asked Lisa.

"Alive, yes, but injured and scared. Jody doesn't feel far away."

Tally followed Lisa's vision until they landed on an outcropping of rock, which led down to the beach. The scene shifted, and she saw Jody climbing the outcropping. She watched as he bent down to pick something from the rock, and then he disappeared. "What the heck?"

"I think he slipped into a crevice in the rocks. It looks like he fell several feet and is lodged. His right leg is at an odd angle like maybe it's broken," Lisa replied.

Tally saw him. He had blood stains on both arms from scrapes and cuts from the jagged rock. She flinched when she saw his leg, lodged above a large rock. She reached down and softly stroked his face. "We're coming," she whispered.

"Mom?" he cried out.

"I'm Tally. Your Mom will be here soon. We've got to get Jody out," Tally said. "Thank you, Lisa."

"Anytime, that was an easy one." Lisa smiled and faded into the darkness.

†

Tally stood and walked back to the anxious group. She smiled at Blair. "I think I know where he is," she said to his parents. "Is there an outcropping of rocks that reaches the ocean nearby?"

"Yes, nearly two miles farther up the beach," Sheriff Boone replied.

"He was climbing the outcropping and fell into a crevice. He's scared and injured, but he's okay." Tally looked at Jody's Mom. "I think he may have a broken leg and some cuts and scrapes, but he's going to be okay. He looks wedged in between rocks, so you may need some equipment."

"I'll get the fire department rolling. You two can ride with me," Sheriff Boone said.

"Thank you so much," June said, and grabbed Tally in a hug.

"You're welcome. Let's go get Jody."

The sheriff barked an order to halt the search and led Tally and Blair to her truck. Jody's parents followed behind in their car. She radioed dispatch for an ambulance to respond to the scene. She looked over at Tally. "That was freaking amazing."

Blair looked at Tally. "You okay?"

"I will be once he's rescued," Tally replied.

"We are so lucky you two came on vacation here," Sheriff Boone said. "It may have taken several more hours for us to reach this spot, on foot. I can't imagine how scared he is."

"He's going to be fine. I told him we were coming." Tally smiled.

Tally shivered as a chill passed through her.

"There's a blanket behind the back seat," Boone told Blair. "The temperature is starting to drop."

†

When they arrived at the outcropping, Sheriff Boone parked and started toward the rocks. Blair took a step to follow when Tally, caught her arm. "No, ma'am, you don't. Your shoulder is still healing. The sheriff and her team can rescue him."

"I'm alright, Tally," Blair groaned, itching to join the action.

Tally smiled. "That's how I plan to keep you. Please stay with me."

The Fire Department and Ambulance weren't far behind. Jody's dad, Brian, had joined Sheriff Boone on the rocks. They could see her bent over talking to Jody.

"They've found him," Blair said and wrapped her arm around Tally's blanket clad shoulders.

Jody's mom had joined them, and she looked up with tears streaming down her face. "Thank you so much for finding our Jody. He's our only child."

"We are happy to help whenever we can," Tally said and took her hand. "He's going to be okay." She smiled to June. "He's worried you'll be mad at him. He broke his phone during the fall."

"Silly boy. He was due for a new one anyhow." She smiled back at Tally.

†

They moved between the parked vehicles to shelter from the wind and to make room for the emergency crews to bring equipment through. The firemen used the Jaws of Life machine to pry the crevice walls apart enough to safely ease Jody from his confinement. He cried out in pain when his leg was touched, but he was on his way out of the crack. He was transferred on to a backboard and then carried up to a waiting gurney. June rushed to his side and held his hand as they prepared him for transport.

"Where is she?" he asked.

"Where is who, honey?" June asked.

"Tally, the woman who talked to me."

June's eyes shot to Tally, and she waved her over.

Tally and Blair walked over to him. He smiled up at Tally. "You're Tally, aren't you?"

Tally reached down to stroke his cheek. "Yes, I am, and I'm very proud of you for being so brave."

"Thank you for finding me." He grimaced at the pain in his leg.

"You're very welcome. You're safe now. You just focus on getting better, okay?"

"Yes, ma'am," he said with a forced smile.

"Are you riding with us, ma'am?" a paramedic asked.

"Yes," she answered and nodded. "I won't leave you."

"I'll follow behind," Brian told them. "I'm so glad you're safe, son."

"Me too, dad. That was scary."

The paramedics loaded him into the back of the ambulance and drove off.

"Thanks again," Brian said, and then raced to his car to follow.

†

Sheriff Boone followed the firemen back up to their truck. "Good job, guys, thanks."

"Our pleasure, Sheriff," the captain said. "We needed a good training exercise." He grinned.

"He's going to be okay. As you guessed, he did have a broken leg, and he may need a few stitches here and there. But he'll be going home, that's what is important."

"That's great news," Blair replied.

"Where can I drop you, ladies? It's getting cold fast."

Blair gave her directions back to the beach house.

"If this isn't ironic," the sheriff said as she pulled up to the house.

"What?" Blair asked.

The sheriff pointed to the sign above the address. It read *Colten*. "This house belongs to Jody's family."

"Damn, that is ironic," Blair chuckled.

"Curious," Tally said.

"Thanks for the ride home," Blair said. "I hope Jody will be able to go home tonight."

"I think he will. He's got new guardian angels watching out for him. When do you head home?"

"The day after tomorrow," Blair replied. "We want to try to come back for a week at Christmas, though. It's so beautiful and relaxing here."

"Drop in for a visit if you make it back. I will do my best to not make you work. Have a great rest of your evening, ladies."

"Thanks," Blair replied.

Tally folded the blanket and placed it on the seat. "That was a lifesaver," she told Sheriff Boone.

"For a lifesaver." Sheriff Boone winked at Tally. "Your skills are amazing."

"Thanks. Goodnight, Sheriff."

†

Blair wrapped Tally in her arms as they watched the sheriff pull away. They stood on the deck watching the white breakers against the dark night. The smell of salt in the air and the sound of the waves was relaxing. They had only been home a few minutes when Blair started laughing.

"What is so funny?" Tally asked. She wiped away something that brushed against her cheek.

"It's snowing," Blair said.

"What?" Another flake landed on her cheek and melted. "Damn, you're right," she chuckled.

The snow continued to fall as they walked back into the house they had rented. Blair lit a fire in the fireplace, and they made love for hours.

†

The ground was covered in a sprinkling of snow the next morning.

"Too bad we leave tomorrow. I bet this place is gorgeous blanketed in snow." Blair sighed.

"I do hope we get to come back," Tally said.

"That sounds like a wonderful idea. Maybe Christmas through New Year's?" Blair suggested.

Tally nodded and smiled. "I'll check to see if this place is available then," Blair replied.

†

Blair was at the stove preparing to make pancakes when there was a knock at the door. She looked at Tally, who was sipping coffee, and shrugged. "I have no clue who that could be." She walked to the door to find Jody and his parents standing there.

"Well, hello," Blair said. "Come on in." She held the door wide for the visitors.

"You're doing great on those crutches, young man," Tally said, causing Jody to grin.

"Come in and have a seat. I was just preparing pancakes if you'd like to join us?" Blair said.

"Thanks, but we stopped for an early breakfast on the way home from the hospital," Brian said. "I hope you don't mind the intrusion, but Jody wanted to say thank you and ask you to be the first to sign his cast."

"Would you?" Jody asked and handed a pen to Tally.

"I'd love to," Tally said. She smiled at him.

"You know, I thought I was crazy last night, but you do have different colored eyes," he said. "They are really cool."

"Thanks, Jody. Some people get a bit freaked out by them."

"Not me. Is that how you could see me last night?" he asked.

Tally pulled the top off the pen. "It has something to do with it. I always felt different when I was a kid and could see things other people couldn't. The summer I turned twelve, I

202

spent my days riding my bike, looking for coke bottles to return for a refund. I got caught up in a thunderstorm one day and got struck by lightning." She lifted the sleeve of her arm to show him the scar. "That really helped me to understand my gift of second sight. Since then, I understood what it was and wasn't afraid to use it to help people."

"I am so glad you were here to help me last night," Jody said. "I was really scared."

"I know you were. But now you're home safe and sound and have a cool cast for your friends to sign and draw on." She snapped the cap back on the pen. "There you go."

He looked at her signature and the funny angel she had drawn. "Thanks! That's so cool." He turned to Blair. "Would you mind?"

"I'd love to be next," Blair answered.

June cleared her throat. "Sheriff Boone told us you were renting the house last night when she came to the hospital. The payment for this visit has already been processed, but she mentioned that you would like to spend Christmas and New Year's here."

Blair's head shot up. "We'd love to if the house is available. We love this spot."

Brian quickly replied. "It is available, and we want to give you that time cost-free for what you did for our family."

"That's not necessary," Blair said.

"It is for us. There's no way we could ever repay you for saving our little man. Jody has also requested that you two come join us for Christmas dinner."

"Please," Jody said.

Blair looked to Tally for confirmation. Tally smiled and nodded. "We'd love to join you if it's no trouble."

June smiled. "No trouble at all. We can confirm the time when you two get back up here. Just don't forget to put us on your calendar."

"Oh, we won't. We can't wait to come back up." Blair assured her.

"Thanks, we'll get out of your hair now so you can have breakfast. Thanks again for everything," June said.

Jody hobbled over to Tally and kissed her on the cheek. "See you soon," he grinned.

"Be careful and watch out for cracks," Tally teased him.

Blair walked them to the door, and turned back to Tally. "That was really sweet. That was a very generous offer of them too. I guess we have those holidays planned. What are we doing for Thanksgiving?"

"I thought I would fly Mom up for the holiday, and the four of us could celebrate together," Tally replied.

"You wouldn't be playing a bit of matchmaker, would you?" Blair teased.

"What's not to love about the Coopers?" Tally asked innocently and batted her eyelashes at Blair.

"Great answer," Blair said. "Let me whip up this batter, and we can eat."

"Sounds perfect," Tally said and poured a fresh cup.

†

Two weeks after their return, Blair received the *All Clear* to return to work. They had both enjoyed the time together during Blair's convalescence, but Tally knew Blair was ready to get back to work.

Her Director, though, thought otherwise. He booked her several speaking engagements at the Academy and also some state law enforcement conferences.

As the weeks began slipping away toward December, Blair scheduled a meeting to discuss attending Caruso's execution and a Christmas vacation.

The Director relented on the Bureau footing the bill for her and Tally to fly to Texas for the execution. "I reckon that's the least I can do since the bastard tried to kill you."

"I don't have a problem footing the bill," Blair assured him.

"No, if you're going as an FBI representative, the Bureau should pay for it. You put in a lot of hard work to get him on death row and then track down another ten victims. You need to be there."

"Thank you, sir."

"You've got a ton of vacation time to use as well. The Jody Colten story was good PR for the agency, and I'd love to hear how he's getting along. Take whatever time you want. I can't promise we won't call, but I'll try my best."

"I understand when duty calls, I have to go."

"Duty is calling now. Go get ready for the Academy speech you need to give this graduating class. I'll have the flights and hotel arrangements made for Texas. In the day before and out the day after?"

"That's perfect. We'll have time for brisket and some chicken-fried steak," Blair teased.

"Your dad raves about that brisket. Bring me some back if you can, so I can judge for myself."

"You got it," Blair said and left his office.

Tally was waiting in her office when Blair returned. "We are a go for Texas and vacation. I promised to bring some brisket back for the Director, though."

"Why don't we just go online and order some sent to him overnight?" Tally suggested.

Blair grinned at her. "You say I'm the smart one. Can you do that while I work on this damn speech?"

Tally chuckled. "Sure. Ten pounds?"

"That should butter him up well unless Dad gets wind he's got brisket."

"I can keep a secret," Tally said, and crossed her heart.

CHAPTER TWELVE

Blair scratched her head. "For the life of me, I can't remember what I did with that wedding band," she told Tally.

"I can," Tally said as she entered the room. "You left it in the pocket of your shorts when we left the hospital. I found it when I was doing laundry." She walked over to Blair's desk and opened a drawer. "It's right here."

"Thanks, sweetie," Blair took the ring from her. "I don't know what I'd do without you."

"Have you decided to give it to him?" Tally asked.

"I don't know, but I need to take it. I don't want any memory of Caruso in our home."

"Baby, I don't think that's going to be entirely possible. You will always have the scar from the gunshot as a reminder."

"Now you're just impossible, Tally," Blair said. "The ring is a different story. I had thoughts of holding it up as he's strapped down on the execution table, but that doesn't seem right. A small part of me wants to taunt him, but the better part of me says to give it to the warden to have put on his hand afterward. What do you think?"

"I'll admit taunting would maybe be more satisfying, but I also remember what you said in the hospital," she replied.

"Oh Lord, what did I say?" Blair asked.

"That if you gave it to Caruso, you would be admitting defeat. He has not defeated you, so I'd go with plan B. He doesn't need to know you even have it."

"Have you changed your mind about going to the execution?" Blair asked.

"I do not wish to attend, but if you need me to, I'll be right there by your side," Tally answered.

"No, I don't think it's necessary. I believe Linda and maybe Jamie will be there."

"I got an email from him yesterday. He's applied for a transfer to Texas. If for some odd reason, he gets denied by the Bureau, he's going to apply for the Texas Rangers."

Blair shook her head. "The Texas Bureau would be foolish not to accept him. He's a sharp young man and has the makings of a great agent."

"Yes, I agree. It may be easier on a new relationship though if Jamie and Linda don't work at the same agency. Whichever they decide, I hope they make it as a couple."

"They are kind of cute together, aren't they?" Blair smiled. "They complement one another's styles, too. Who knew Linda could play such a good, bad cop?"

"She is tough as nails. I still chuckle when I think of how she handled the coroner when you got shot. I couldn't have done better myself."

Tally noticed that Blair had the ring in her hand, and she was spinning it between her fingers. "Tell me where you're packing that, so I'll know where to remind you to look." She chuckled as she pointed to the ring.

"You take it, so I won't need to ask," Blair said and handed it to Tally.

"Okay, I'm going to store it in my hygiene bag. Just in case I forget." Tally winked and took the ring. She walked into the bedroom and packed it away. "I do hope Jamie attends, so we can see him again. I'm sure he'd love some brisket and chicken-fried." She laughed.

"Do you think I should go ahead and pack the bags in the car tonight?" Blair asked.

"That's one less thing we'll have to do in the morning. We only have one big bag and a smaller one," Tally said. "We're only going to be there two nights."

"That's right. Tomorrow and Saturday night, then home on Sunday. Then we can start counting the days until we leave for Christmas."

"It will be less than two weeks," Tally reminded her. "I still need help figuring out what to get Jody as a gift."

"Have you reached out to June for an idea?" Blair suggested.

"That would be entirely too practical," Tally said. "I'll email her in the morning."

"You know what may be an idea?" Blair asked.

"I'm open to anything."

"He likes beachcombing for treasures, so how about a metal detector?"

Tally's eyes lit up. "That's perfect, I'll ask June if he has one already or if that would be a good gift for Jody. Great idea, babe."

"I do have my moments." Blair chuckled and took Tally in her arms for a kiss.

†

"I think I'm finally getting used to this," Tally said as she relaxed back in her seat. "Flying isn't so bad after all."

Blair reached over for Tally's hand. "I still enjoy a beautiful drive, but it's convenient when you need to get somewhere fast."

"That's for sure." Tally entwined her fingers with Blair's. "Mom sure had a good time at Thanksgiving. I think we should invite her up more often."

Blair patted her stomach. "I don't know if my waistline can handle that. Lord, that woman can cook."

"I'd be more than happy to help you work the calories off." Tally wiggled her eyebrows.

"Can she come up next weekend then?"

"I think it might be a bit too soon. I think Mom and Thomas hit it off pretty well, don't you?"

"Yes, they seemed to have quite a lot to talk about. Mostly stories about us from the sound of it, but I guess that's normal for parents to discuss their kids."

Blair watched as Tally closed her eyes and drifted off to sleep. Her thoughts turned to Casper Caruso and how he felt on his final days on earth. He was despicable and deserved a much less humane end than he gave his victims, but there would be no more destruction from him. Unfortunately, she knew for every serial killer that was captured, a few more would take their place. The world was an evil place. Blair was nearly asleep when she felt Tally twitch. She looked over at her lover to find her sleeping peacefully and probably dreaming from the look of the smile on her face. Blair loved it when Tally had pleasant dreams. So many of her visions were filled with violence and fear, she was happy for a brief respite. Blair closed her eyes and enjoyed the feel of Tally's hand clasped in hers.

†

They were both jarred awake when the jet landed. "Damn, that was a bumpy arrival," Blair groaned as she sat up.

"Not the best ending to a smooth flight, but we're safely on the ground. Did you nap, too?"

"Yes, I did. I used to get some of my best sleep on flights," Blair chuckled. "You looked like you were dreaming."

"I was having the most delightful dreams of us in front of the fireplace in Maine. I'm really looking forward to our return trip."

Blair squeezed Tally's hand. "I am, too. It can't get here quick enough."

211

Tally's phone pinged, and she glanced at it. "June says a metal detector would be an excellent gift for Jody." Tally's nose scrunched up. "How are we going to get one up there on a jet?"

"I think we can find a local store in Maine online and have it ready for pick up. Or we can ask the good sheriff if we could have it shipped to her." Blair chuckled. Rebecca Boone and her wife, Susan, had invited them out for New Year's and had started emailing them often. Susan, an RN at the local hospital, planned a small dinner before ringing in the New Year and watching the fireworks from their home near the beach. "You know we're going to have to schedule a summer trip up there. The clambakes sure sound like a lot of fun. Not so much in the winter, though."

Tally nodded. "That sounds good to me. Anything with lobster and clams grabs my attention."

Blair stood and retrieved the carry-on bag from the overhead and placed it in her seat. "I'll collect my sidearm and meet you at the car rental spot if you'll get our suitcase from baggage claim."

"Easy peasy," Tally replied. "When are we supposed to meet Linda for dinner?"

"At five," Blair replied.

"That should give us time to check into the hotel and freshen up a bit." Tally smiled. "I'll see you in a few minutes."

Blair watched as Tally walked toward the baggage claim, then she turned to retrieve her sidearm.

"Welcome back, Agent Cooper," the security officer said as she signed for her weapon.

"Thanks. It's great to be back in Texas." Blair replied.

"Are you here for the execution?" he softly asked.

"Yes, I am. Has it been big news this week?"

"Damned protesters at the prison gate. You know how they are. They don't give a damn about the victims, just the criminal's poor, unfortunate soul," he growled.

Blair shook her head. "I will never understand them. I wish I could have an hour to share some of the photos and other grisly details of the crimes he committed. Maybe then they would understand how easily Caruso is getting off compared to his victims."

"I appreciate all that you do to take creeps like him off the streets. Our world is a killing field as it is without adding a serial killer to the mix."

"Ain't that the truth?" Blair placed her weapon in her shoulder rig. She winced from an ache in her shoulder.

The security officer saw her expression. "Does it still hurt?"

"Aches like a bitch on cold and wet days," she smiled.

"Well, it will be warm and dry while you're here. So says the weatherman, but you know how often they are wrong." He chuckled.

"Thanks. Will you be here Sunday?" she asked.

"No, ma'am, I'm off with the missus." He grinned. "Have a safe flight home."

"Thanks, you keep safe, too," Blair said with a smile and, with a wave, she turned to leave. She made it three steps before she spun around and returned for the carry-on bag. "Let's try this again." She grinned at the officer.

†

213

Tally handed Blair the keys after the luggage was stored. "What? You don't want to drive?" Blair teased.

"No, ma'am, the pleasure to be my chauffeur is all yours."

Blair took the keys from her. "I'll drive you anywhere you want to go."

Tally pulled out her sunglasses. "Damn, it seems unusually bright out today."

"It's Texas, Darlin', the sun burns brighter here." She winked. "Are you hungry?"

"A bit, but I'm going to save my appetite for that chicken-fried tonight. Maybe I can finish the portion this trip."

"Ha! Good luck with that. I'd suggest we split one, but that doesn't leave me any leftovers."

"Have no fear. If Jamie comes you won't have to worry about wasting food."

Blair chuckled as they drove to the hotel. "That never gets old." She pointed out a pasture in the middle of a subdivision with dozens of longhorn cattle grazing. "You don't see that in Virginia."

Tally smiled. "No, you don't."

†

Tally moaned when they entered the room. "Why do they have to make the rooms so danged cold?" She walked to the thermostat and adjusted it to seventy-two.

"Feels pretty darn good to me," Blair said.

"Uh, huh, if we're snuggled under that down comforter, and I'm next to your super-hot body." Tally turned and kissed Blair.

Blair's phone pinged with a text. *We'll pick you up at the hotel at five.* "Well, so I guess Jamie did make it." Tally smiled.

Perfect. We can't wait to see you two. Blair added a smiley face.

"We have an hour. Do you want to kick back and relax?" Tally asked as she picked up the remote to the television.

A local news station was running a breaking news report, showing the crowd of protesters at Huntsville Penitentiary.

"Good grief," Tally said and turned up the volume to listen to the reporter's story.

"A large crowd has begun to gather outside of the prison to protest the scheduled execution of serial killer Casper Caruso, also named the Ghost of East Texas. Caruso was convicted on six murders and recently connected with another ten victims, including his wife, whom Caruso killed and then framed an innocent man for her murder. The crowd is carrying signs and chanting for the Governor to commute his sentence to life in prison. Officials at the prison and the Governor's office have offered no comments. The execution is scheduled for tomorrow night at six pm. Stay tuned for more local news."

"At least they didn't flash his picture all over the place." Blair groaned.

"Do you think his sentence may be commuted?" Tally asked.

"Not a snowball's chance in hell, or Texas for that matter." She lowered the volume. "Caruso asked for an execution date when his final appeal was denied. He could have sat on death row for several more years, but he enjoys being in control of his destiny. I'm sure he's enjoying the protesters' attention immensely."

"No doubt. I'll be glad when this is all over."

"Very soon, my love. Very soon." Blair took Tally's hand in hers and kissed it. "Is it five yet?"

Tally smirked. "You getting hungry, too?"

"Yeah. I'm gonna text Linda to come early if they are ready."

†

Over dinner, Jamie updated them on his progress in moving to Texas. "I've been accepted by both agencies."

"Do you really want to leave the Bureau?" Blair asked.

"No, not really. Linda and I have discussed the added pressure of working in the same agency, and we think we can handle it."

"There's your answer then. If it doesn't work out, then you have a backup plan."

Tally smiled at Jamie. "It's worked out well so far for us, but I know it's different for y'all. You'll have to work hard to not bring the work home with you, and find stuff you like to do together."

"We've already discussed a few options for hobbies we can do together," Linda replied. "Hunting and four-wheeling were easy, but convincing him to try golf is a different story."

"Just let him drive you around in the golf cart until he realizes how much fun it is," Blair suggested.

"I just don't see anything fun about whacking a little ball all over the place to get it in a tiny hole," Jamie groaned.

Tally smirked at him. "Is that it, or are you're afraid Linda will be better than you?"

"There is that," he admitted.

"I've been playing for years," Linda said and punched him in the shoulder. "You're a natural athlete, and I think you would be a good player if you tried. If not, I guess I'll have to take those clubs I bought you for Christmas back."

"What? You already bought me clubs?" Jamie asked.

"Yep, I snuck in your measurements when you were sleeping and had a set made for you," Linda replied. "No problem, though. I'm sure the store can find some other gorgeous, six-foot-three man to use them."

"Oh, goodness, Jamie. I wanna see you work your way out of that one," Blair teased.

"Golf it is then," he smiled and kissed Linda. "Are we on for brisket tomorrow?" he asked Blair.

"Is it hot outside?" Blair shot back at him. "We had ten pounds sent to our Director, and he was purring like a kitten when he got it."

"I'll have to remember that," Linda said. She looked at Tally. "I heard you had some excitement while you were in Maine."

Tally told them the story about helping to rescue Jody.

"Can you work remotely? I mean, like if sent you something, could you use it to locate someone?" Jamie asked.

"That all depends. If the person is still alive, their energy is more reliable, and it's easier for me to connect, but if they are deceased, it can be more difficult. I'd be willing to give it a try if you ever need me," she told him. "Both of you."

Blair grinned. "We're getting the evil eye from the waitress. I think she needs this table. Would y'all like to come back to the room with us?"

Jamie checked the time. "Are you sure it's not too late?"

Tally chuckled, "We both napped on the flight. Besides, we can sleep in tomorrow."

"Great, we've both missed you since you left," Linda said.

†

"Would you two be interested in sharing a few beers with us?" Jamie asked as he pulled out of the parking lot.

"Yeah, we can do that," Blair answered.

"Michelob Ultra okay for y'all?" Linda asked.

"Perfect," Tally replied.

†

Jamie and Linda sat on the small loveseat while Blair took the recliner and Tally stretched out on the bed.

"What did you decide on about the wedding band?" Jamie asked

"Well, the airlines wouldn't allow me to open a window to toss it out, so I had to bring it. I won't be giving it to Caruso before his execution. I want him to know I bested him in every way. That may sound arrogant, but that's how I feel."

"I don't blame you one bit." Jamie shrugged. "I'm not sure I would return it at all."

"I'll give it to the Warden afterward to have placed on him, but I won't give him the comfort of knowing he will be wearing it to his grave."

"That's very understandable, honey." Tally smiled.

"The ironic part is that he will be placed in a pauper's grave if no family shows up to claim him," Linda informed him. "His last known relative, his alcoholic father, passed away last year. No one else is expected to claim him. No service, no prayers, no mourners. Just a cheap coffin, no glory."

"Sad way for anybody to leave this world, but where he's headed, he'll get a warm welcome," Tally stated.

Blair's head whipped around to look at Tally then back to Linda and Jamie. "Did you just hear that come out of her mouth?" she teased.

"I did, but I thought I misheard it," Jamie replied. "Tally made a funny." He giggled like a school kid.

Everyone joined him in laughter. "You never cease to amaze me, Tally Rainwater," Blair told her.

The twelve pack ran out around eleven.

"I guess we should head out," Jamie said. "Do you want us to pick y'all up tomorrow for brisket?"

"Yes, if you don't mind, around two, then we can drop Tally back here and head out to the prison. If I can see the warden beforehand, I'll give him the wedding band so we can leave right after."

"You're not going, Tally?" Jamie asked.

"No, I don't plan to. Blair will have the two of you there. I really don't want to see him again."

Jamie nodded. "No problem at all. We'll see the deed done, and then we can grab a bite to eat. We've found a great steak place if you want to try something different. They have the most amazing Brussels sprouts."

Blair chuckled at his exuberance. "That sounds good."

†

The beer had relaxed Tally, and she found it hard to keep her eyes open. Blair took her in her arms. "What do you say we get a nice long sleep tonight, have a late breakfast, and just chill tomorrow?"

"Sounds great to me. That beer hit me harder than I expected."

"I love you, my little lightweight," Blair said, and kissed her softly.

†

When they returned to the room after breakfast, the housekeeper had already straightened their room. "I will bring out the laptop if you text Becca and see if we can ship a metal detector to her," Tally said.

"You, my love, have a deal."

Tally set up the laptop and began browsing the internet. "Oh, this one looks good and is adjustable, which would be great as he grows taller."

"You are assuming he will enjoy using it?" Blair said.

"Of course, he will. He loves treasure hunting and his guardian angels," Tally replied.

They looked at a few other options but kept returning to the one. "Are we in agreement this is the one we should buy?" Blair asked.

"Yes, I think so. The bright lime-green one," she smiled.

"I'm so glad you didn't say the hot pink one," Blair hit the button to order.

"I wouldn't mind having that one for our beach trips," Tally hinted.

"Merry Christmas, baby," Blair said and ordered a second one, shipping it to their home address.

"That will be so much fun," Tally said. "You can sit under the umbrella and read while I go on a scavenger hunt."

"Now who says I won't join you?" Blair said. "I just need a little more extended model. Shucks, no hot pink. Can you live with me having a chrome one?"

"Absolutely," Tally smiled.

†

"I'll book our flights while y'all are gone," she told Blair when she was dropped back at the hotel after lunch.

Blair nodded. "That sounds perfect. See you soon."

Jamie waited for Tally to enter the hotel then pulled off.

"Have either of you been to an execution?" Blair asked.

"Nope, it's a first for both of us," Linda answered.

"Lethal injection is much easier to witness. The individual gets strapped down, sedated, and then given a dose of medicine to stop his heart. Much cleaner and faster than the electric chair."

"I don't regret not seeing one by electrocution," Jamie replied.

"I just wonder what he has to say before they start the procedure," Blair said.

"I reckon we will find out soon," Linda said.

†

Armed guards had to clear a path for Jamie to enter. A group of twenty or so protesters surrounded the vehicle as he drove through the crowd. Blair saw one particular young man, dressed in black near the center of the group. His pale skin drew attention to his dark eyes. When she locked eyes with him, he grinned, and Blair knew he was evil. She could feel it flowing from him, feeding the frenzy of the crowd.

"I'll be back for you one day," she murmured.

Linda thought Blair had said something from the back seat. "Did you say something, Blair?"

"The young goth-looking, kid. Did you see him?"

"With the dark hollow eyes?" Linda asked.

"Yeah, that's the one, pure evil. We will be hunting for him one day. He's got serial killer stamped all over him."

"I bet you're right," Jamie said after getting a glimpse of him. "Can you snap a quick photo, Linda?"

Linda snapped a photo as the young man extended his middle finger. "Yep, that's the one."

"You might want to get a list of anyone who has corresponded with Caruso. For every one convicted, at least two are spawned. On your slow days, you can start eliminating potential suspects until you narrow the list down to possible perps, then flag them for monitoring. You may save us all some hard work and family heartaches if we can intervene quicker."

"I would have never thought of that," Linda said. "It makes perfect sense, though."

Blair had a sadness in her voice. "Bobby Joiner was just the first. I'm almost certain there will be others."

†

They were checked into the witness room and took seats near the front. Blair recognized several family members of victims from the trial, and she nodded to them. There was no emotional energy to smile, and it wouldn't lessen their pain. Jamie and Linda chose to sit on either side of her. She felt they were attempting to shroud her from the hate and negative energy they felt so strongly in the room.

She watched the clock on the wall count down toward six. The door to the chamber opened, and Caruso, still shackled, was led inside to sit in a chair. A small microphone was placed in front of him.

Caruso's eyes scanned the room, his smile growing as he saw the hate-filled eyes glaring back at him. When he found Blair, he leaned forward.

"I'm sad Tally didn't join you today, Special Agent Cooper. Send her my regards." Blair nodded as heads turned toward her. Caruso lifted his hand and pointed to his finger. Blair shrugged and watched his facial expression fall from smug to near rage.

He turned away from her quickly. "I won't tell you I'm sorry," he said to the families, "because I'm not. I don't think I have the capacity for remorse."

"Go ahead and kill the bastard," a man shouted from the crowd.

"He has to have his say," one of the prison guards announced.

Caruso turned back to Blair. "You won this round, but I am far from done."

Blair's expression did not change to react to his statement. She knew he was right. There would always be more. She simply nodded and smiled.

"Let's get this done," Caruso growled when he realized he would not be getting a response from Blair or her team.

They watched stoically as he was led to the gurney and strapped into place. An IV line was inserted, and the sedative administered. Caruso's body went limp, and his eyes closed. At six pm sharp, the warden nodded to the doctor, and the lethal dose was injected into Caruso's arm. Caruso's body flexed once as it reacted to fight the medication to stop his heart, and then he fell quiet once more. After several minutes, the doctor pulled out a stethoscope to listen for a pulse. When he determined Caruso's heartbeat would not return, he nodded to the warden, and the blinds were closed. A voice came across the speaker announcing the death at nine minutes after six.

The crowd began to filter out. Blair, Jamie, and Linda were some of the last to leave.

As they walked out to the SUV, they saw two young men who had remained after the crowd of protesters had disbanded after the pronouncement: the dark-clad figure, and a young man, clean-cut, who looked like a cowboy just off a cattle drive. They glared across the parking lot, and Jamie snapped a couple more photos.

"Brazen little bastards," he growled when they climbed into the vehicle.

"Definitely two to watch if you can determine who they are," Blair said. "They may not be on your radar now, but they will be eventually." She sighed. "It may not hurt to look into who Bobby Joiner's acquaintances were as well."

Jamie started out of the lot, and one of the men picked up a rock and threw it but missed the vehicle.

"Punk ass throws like a girl," Jamie growled.

"Hey, now. I would have hit something this big easily."

"Sorry, ladies. Old phrases die hard."

Blair grinned at Linda. "No problem. Both of you send me those pictures, and I'll see what I can find out from my end."

Linda took Jamie's phone and forwarded his photos and then hers to Blair. "There you go."

"Thanks. How far from the hotel is the steak place? Do we need to follow you?" Blair asked.

"It's not far at all," Jamie replied. "If you want to call Tally, we can go by and pick her up. I hear red meat calling to me."

Blair noticed that Jamie kept an eye on the rearview mirror in case the punks tried to follow them.

†

Jamie wasn't exaggerating about the quality of the steak house, and the portions were Texas-sized. After the delicious meal, they returned to the hotel. Saying goodbye to the two young agents was just as hard the second go around, but Blair felt like they would be seeing them again.

She stripped out of her work attire and into a pair of sleep pants and a T-shirt while Tally pulled on an oversized shirt.

Tally climbed into her arms. "You haven't said much about the execution. Did everything go, okay?"

"Relatively so. Caruso is history, but I'm afraid we met two of his disciples today."

"What?" Tally replied.

"Two young men who had taken part in the protest." She picked up her phone and showed Tally the photographs. "The one in black emits pure evil, but it's the clean-cut kid that worries me the most. He looks like your average Texan kid. Like a cowboy who just stepped off a horse or tractor. He could hide in plain sight, and no one would suspect him of being a monster in the making."

"That's not good news. Is there anything we can do?"

"Linda and Jamie are going to do some research into Caruso's correspondence while he was in prison, and look into Bobby Joiner's acquaintances to see if we can start putting some names together to monitor."

"Which reminds me, I need to add something to their assignments." She called Jamie and put him on speaker.

"Hey, Blair, do you miss me already?" he teased.

"I do, but talking with Tally sparked an idea I'd like y'all to pursue."

"What's that?" They heard Linda ask from the background.

"See if the prison scanned Caruso's correspondence, incoming and outgoing. We may be able to decipher some clues from them. If you get them, send them to me, and I can work on them, too."

"I'll get on it first thing Monday, no wait, I'll call the warden tonight. I still have his cell number," Linda answered. "I don't know how long they will keep his records after his execution."

"Good point. Ask the warden if we can have the originals or at least a copy if they planned to destroy them," Blair said.

"I'm on it. I'll keep you posted," Linda replied.

"Thanks, guys. Enjoy the rest of your weekend." Blair ended the call.

"No more shop talk," Tally said, and convinced Blair with a slow, deep kiss.

Ali Spooner

EPILOGUE

The return trip to Maine for Christmas was fantastic. Jody loved his gift and insisted they join him the next day to do some beachcombing. He found many coins and even someone's class ring from 1982. He was ecstatic with every little find, and his excitement spread to Blair and Tally.

"All this excitement makes me want to go to our beach when we get home," Tally said.

"Not only the beach, but we've got battlefields and all kinds of other sites we can explore."

"I hadn't even thought about those, Blair."

†

Becca and Susan were fantastic hosts, the dinner and company were terrific. After the New Year was rung in, the couples exchanged a toast to Twenty-Twenty.

Susan and Tally walked to the railing as the fireworks began. Becca and Blair poured fresh drinks. Becca smiled at Blair. "I hope y'all have a great year."

Blair sighed. "I'm grateful the events are over in Texas for now, but I fear this will be a hell of a year. With it being an election year and the rising bile of hate being spewed out of our capital and major cities, I think we will have our hands full."

Becca nodded. "Here's to surviving the wrath of that to come." She raised her glass and clicked it with Blair's as the fireworks popped and lit up the sky. "Let's go join our ladies to start the New Year right."

ABOUT ALI SPOONER

Ali Spooner lives in beautiful northwest Florida with her long-term partner and several fur babies. Ali's writing began as a hobby, and with the assistance of the Affinity Rainbow Publishing team has advanced her love of storytelling to a new level.

Ali's characters are primarily everyday people, from cowgirls to psychics. Ali also has created a few supernatural characters in her paranormal series. Several of her twenty-plus books have been Amazon-rated number one choices and always include a happily ever after. Ali's hobbies include photography, reading, travel, college sports, and spending time with family and friends.

OTHER AFFINITY BOOKS

Terminal Event—Ali Spooner

Tally Rainwater was born with the gift of second sight, something she never understood. A near-fatal accident, at age twelve, makes her visions clearer, but not the reason for them. As she matures, Lisa, a spirit, enters her visions to guide her in using her gift, but still not the reason why. Can Tally and Blair's budding romance survive the possibility? Read this intense murder mystery romance and find out.

The Star Child by Ali Spooner

Eli and Whit are enjoying their life together on the mountain when Whit is called into action for a secret mission at the Pentagon. While she is gone, the Cast Iron Farm comes to life, literally, when Eli discovers a mysterious cave that has a connection to Whit's past. Younger brother Brad joins the gang. When Whit returns, she plans an Appalachian Trail adventure with Brad and Mitch. Join Eli and family as their adventure at Cast Iron Farm continues.

<u>My Dear Vet by JM Dragon</u>
Ava Lawrence, a research veterinarian, is thrown in the deep end when her uncle asks her to cover his country practice while he has a vacation of a lifetime. How could she refuse? His team shouldn't be any different than the crew at her parents' practice, oh, was she so wrong. What she now has to work with is a sassy nurse, an obnoxious receptionist, and an animal whisperer, or so it seems. Ava finds herself embroiled in taking care of animals in the area and local issues outside her experience, making her question her sanity. Throw in chickens, cats, dogs, and a donkey named Theo, along with various other animals. This turns out to be Ava's unexpected adventure with far reaching romantic benefits.

<u>One Shot at Love</u> by Annette Mori
Blair returns to her hometown after the death of her sister. Always an activist she vows to use her voice to advocate for better gun control. She meets Maribel, an irresistible, sexy woman who proves to be an enigma to Blair. Maribel can't help approaching the weeping woman and learning the origin of Blair's grief, Maribel thinks she is the last person who should form a friendship with Blair. Ultimately, the allure is too much for Maribel, but how long can she keep her secret and continue to nurture their burgeoning feelings for one another. A committed left-wing social activist could never fall for the poster child of the NRA. Unless taking that one shot at love matters more than anything else.

<u>The Mountain Whispers</u> by Ali Spooner

Arriving home and discovering the betrayal by her best friend and lover, Eli Fortner leaves to run off her anger and hurt. A chance stop at a convenience store and the purchase of lottery tickets sends Eli's life into a whirlwind of change. Able to now pursue her dreams, Eli heads off to see what else fate has in store for her.

Whit Brewer, Eli's neighbor, is everything Eli never knew she needed and wanted. But can she let go of the betrayal long enough to let Whit in? Thirteen black cats, a baby goat, and Cruz, her furry best friend, join Eli on her adventure, new life, and the possibility of real love.

Charlie by Erin O'Reilly

At fourteen, Hannah Garvin met 'the one,' Charlene Gaines, and her life was never the same. They were inseparable and spent every moment they could together. One day, Charlie left without a word and again, Hannah's life took a dramatic change. Hannah vowed to never fall in love again. When she meets Mick, a new arrival to the small Texas panhandle town near her family's farm, her heart remembers what being in love was like, and yearns for more. Will Hannah let the memory of Charlie go so she can start a new life with Mick? Or will her heart betray her and hold on to her love for Charlie?

Misha's Promise by Renee MacKenzie

Misha Wyatt has settled into a peaceful existence as a healer in Karst, New America. When an airplane crashes in the meadow outside of Karst, Misha hurries to help the pilot. Misha is not expecting the pilot to be alive...or so beautiful. Will her uncontrollable desire to keep the pilot safe be her downfall? Can *they* survive their journey? The last book in the Karst series brings our characters to their physical and emotional limits. Don't miss the culmination of this exciting series!

Heart Strings Attached by Ali Spooner & Annette Mori
Socialite Remy has her world shaken. Bartender Chancy has her orderly life turned around. A mutually beneficial business agreement between Remy and Chancy turns into undeniable attraction. Will the two ignore culture norms to explore their intense desire for each other?

The Panty Thief by Annette Mori
Someone is stealing panties, but who? And why? Joey Hartford is a fourth-year medical student who insists she doesn't have time for a relationship. A new tenant in her apartment building is proving too tempting to ignore. Sabrina is in her final year of her doctoral program and focused on completing her dissertation. Meeting Joey is dangerous for so many reasons. Add a suicidal ex-girlfriend who suddenly reappears in Sabrina's life and Joey's jealous friend-with-benefits, and things get complicated quickly.

Country Living by Jen Silver
Peri Sanderson achieves her dream of moving from London to a cottage in the English countryside with her wife, Karla. Peri sees their future as pastoral while chatting with the locals in a quaint village pub. Sexy urbanite, Karla, has other ideas. Secrets are everywhere. Peri quickly senses something not quite right among her rural neighbours and also with Karla. Temptation, betrayal, and intrigue combine to change

the lives of both women beyond anything they could have imagined.

Before the Light by Samantha Hicks
One year after her long-time partner Meredith's abduction and their subsequent break-up, Kathleen Bowden-Scott's life is spiralling out of control. She meets Bethany Jones and despite an instant attraction Kathleen shies away. In this fast-paced, romantic suspense, lies are exposed and hearts unite as Kathleen and Beth fight for their future.

Wanted for Christmas by JM Dragon
Belle Farrow knew what she wanted for Christmas—work. She had little to offer but a minor degree in cookery and household management. Certainly not enough for a decent chef or housekeeper position. Then she saw an advert in the local newspaper. Wanted: Housekeeper/cook/nanny for the period of Christmas until the New Year. This is Christmas. Perhaps Santa reads the ad column too and pushes a little spirit of the season to that request.

Dreams in a Jar by JM Dragon
When you believe your life is a never-ending spiral of despair and the only personal joy you have is inside a novel, would you grab a chance to hide away in the local bookstore and dream of adventures? Thea's life is about to embark on a journey she never envisioned when local bookstore owner, Marion, is taken ill. Her niece, Sheryl Appleby, takes over the reins and her presence provides Thea the courage to take a leap of faith. Can she embrace the butterfly effect, or are Thea's dreams bottled in a jar forever?

Affinity
Rainbow Publications

eBooks, Print, Free eBooks

Visit our website for more publications available online.

www.affinityrainbowpublications.com

Published by Affinity Rainbow Publications
A Division of Affinity eBook Press NZ LTD
Canterbury, New Zealand

Registered Company 2517228